# Secrets
### of a
# Small Hotel

# Secrets
### of a
# Small Hotel

ELIZABETH COOKE

abbott press

Abbott Press books may be ordered through booksellers or by contacting:

Abbott Press
1663 Liberty Drive
Bloomington, IN 47403
www.abbottpress.com
Phone: 1-866-697-5310

Because of the dynamic nature of the Internet, any web addresses or
links contained in this book may have changed since publication and
may no longer be valid. The views expressed in this work are solely those
of the author and do not necessarily reflect the views of the publisher,
and the publisher hereby disclaims any responsibility for them.

"Secrets of a Small Hotel" is a work of fiction. Names, characters,
places and incidents are the product of the author's imagination
or are used fictitiously. Any resemblance to actual events,
locales, or persons, living or dead, is entirely coincidental.

Certain stock imagery © Thinkstock.
Any people depicted in stock imagery provided by Thinkstock are
models, and such images are being used for illustrative purposes only.

ISBN: 978-1-4582-1823-0 (e)
ISBN: 978-1-4582-1822-3 (sc)
ISBN: 978-1-4582-1824-7 (hc)

Library of Congress Control Number: 2014919888

Printed in the United States of America.

Abbott Press rev. date: 11/24/2014

# Prologue

❦

*Quel bonheur!* Oh happy day!

I am back again at Hotel Marcel, a small hotel in Paris next to the Eiffel Tower, the Champs de Mars, and Les Invalides. And it is the month of May. As an American woman in her sixties, I have been a frequent sojourner at this small hotel over many years. It is a little over six months since I have been here in my little cocoon in Paris, the city that always seduces.

On that earlier visit, I was able to observe from my balcony, the goings on in three specific luxurious apartments across the avenue. When lighted from within at night, I was drawn into the particular dramas unfolding in those three lamp and candlelit settings, finding the personalities revealed irresistible in their every intense interchange.

*Incroyable!*

An intriguing intermingling between the characters in those apartments, and with residents and frequenters of the Hotel Marcel, had taken place six months ago. Unexpected associations evolved; relationships developed – like a handshake across the avenue. From my balcony room and from the salon below, I was able to relish the vibrant life around me, to even be part of it. What fun it had been.

Most of it, but surely not all. Because animosity bloomed in certain cases, and between certain personalities. No. More than animosity – violence and downright hatred. And secrets. So many mysteries were hidden, and left unsolved, all of which puzzle I carried home with me to New York City and relived and dwelled upon, lo these past six months.

However, most important of all, the loving feelings...the sweetness and laughter I experienced...the delicious exchange between embracing people... I hope all of this is here again, still in full flower and strong enough to overcome those miserable persons with their toxic emanations.

At that time, across the avenue, Emile and Sylvie LaGrange lived in grand apartment building 1, with Sylvie's brutal brother Kurt in the attic room above. Sasha Goodwin, a well-known American photographer/bachelor, had resided in apartment building 2. Pierre and Elise Frontenac, a childless, bourgeois French couple, dwelled in apartment building 3, with a distinctive *femme de ménage* named Henriette.

And in and about the hotel there was of course Jean-Luc Marcel, hotelier and owner of the establishment, and Isabella, his new lady love from Spain; René Poignal, police detective and friend of Jean-Luc; Ray Guild, the outlandish and humorous editor of French *Vogue;* an American born Marquise, Sue de Chevigny, an old friend of mine, and of course, *Moi.*

Much activity had taken place, those six months ago, involving fisticuffs, love affairs, a violent dinner party, the randy photographer and his models, the French inspector imitative of American TV's "Law and Order," Sue's crumbling château in the Loire valley, and Ray Guild who introduced me to an artist of enormous charm, of whom I dream about.

Constantly.

It is over four-and-one-half months since I have been close to that artist, Brit, - Ludwig Turner – he, with whom I am so fascinated. His past is yet hidden from me, is unexplained. I want to know more of him, of what makes him who he is and who helped shape him.

We saw each other briefly in New York last Christmas, while he was there for a showing of his work. It was an electric few days, after which I have yearned for his presence. At last I am here now in the city where he lives and works.

Unfortunately, the difficult underbelly that showed its ugly face six months ago on this placid avenue is here too, spring or no, Paris or no, the unpleasant LaGrange ménage with the brutal brother, Kurt, and their little white dog. They even threatened me, if I should return, because I had witnessed from my balcony an incident that landed Kurt in jail. And Sylvie LaGrange, Kurt's sister? She is extremely unforgiving and perhaps equally as disturbed as he.

I am back now at my Hotel Marcel, directly across the street, ready to revisit the secrets from my past visit as best I can and take care against the fearsome.

However, above all, I am within reach of the artist with whom I am so enchanted, for whom I pine.

And it is spring and all that Paris represents is here for the taking.

I intend to do just that.

# Chapter 1

$\sim$ ❦ $\sim$

## My Small Hotel


It is Friday morning, May 1ˢᵗ. I have arrived. I will be here for three precious weeks.

As I enter the familiar lobby with its small check-in desk, behind which stands Jean-Luc Marcel, owner and proprietor of this small hotel, he comes around to greet me with a big embrace.

"Ah, Madame Elizabeth. Again..."

I laugh. "And pretty soon, right? Oh, Jean-Luc, I am so glad to be here ...as always..."

"And, of course, you will be in your suite..." he says with an impish grin. My suite consists of a small pristine bedroom, but with a balcony overlooking the avenue and the Eiffel Tower stands tall for me on the right.

He pulls me into the salon, retrieves a bottle of champagne from the back kitchen refrigerator and two flutes, into which he proceeds to pour the golden, bubbling liquid.

"Tell me, Jean-Luc. Tell me everything that's happened in the last six months. I'm dying to know. How's Isabella? Is all well between you two? And, of course, Sasha? Is the ogre, Kurt, still in jail?" My words are tumbling.

While not mentioning his beautiful Isabella (which takes me by surprise. Is there trouble in paradise?) Jean-Luc proceeds to fill me in on recent events and people about whom I am curious.

Sasha is living now in Hotel Marcel. He cannot return to apartment building 2, fourth floor duplex, because, when he lived there before, it was illegal to have a darkroom and photography business in a residential building. He is now persona non grata in that building.

He has rented, for work, a small photo studio over the *tabac* shop on Avenue Bosquet where his models still throw off their clothes as he mounts them, I would assume. That surely must have remained the same – his modus sexual vivendi.

Instead, there is an English woman, named Jillian Spenser, divorced, a painter, who moved into Sasha's old duplex in apartment 2, on the fourth and fifth floors, across the street. She has a young daughter about 11 years old named Amelia.

"And Isabella?" I ask softly as he pauses in his narration.

Jean-Luc looks at me, almost blushes and merely nods his head. "You will be seeing her soon. She is delighted you are going to be here for a bit...so eager to see you," he says, his tone subdued.

"And you remember the artist...Ludwig Turner?" I say. "We had dinner together the night before I left last fall."

"You call him Brit... because his mother is British...am I right?"

"Yes."

"What an interesting fellow....and most interested in you, I think," Jean-Luc says with a smile. "But he is American, no?"

"Yes," I say again, pleased with his observation. "He is here in Paris. At his studio in the Marais district." With this thought my heart quickens.

I rise to go up to the fifth floor 'suite' and the first thing I do is phone Brit, as we had arranged. My voice sounds tremulous as I call my new potential *amour* in his atelier, readying a show to be held at a premiere gallery on rue Faubourg St. Honoré.

We are to meet, "as soon as you have revived from jet-lag... your call, my love," he says in that husky voice, as I let him know I have arrived.

And I drop on the inviting bed with a sigh, kicking off my shoes and relishing the soft pillow, but only for a moment. I must go outside to my balcony on this sparkling day and look at the icon of Paris – to really know I'm here. And there it is, as I go through the French doors to the little perch above the treetops that line the avenue. The Eiffel Tower.

I look around to view the three familiar apartments where I have observed many a drama with a sense of familiarity, curiosity, and anticipation. They are all still there in all their art deco beauty, yet what hidden secrets live inside?

I see from the balcony that the Frontenacs in apartment building 3 seem to be intact. I assume old *femme de ménage*, Henriette, still presides. Through their dining room window, I can see that the table, broken up in that fight last fall, is there again, in one piece, and shining.

Emile LaGrange. Sylvie LaGrange. Kurt Vronsky! Lord! What a trio. Sylvie's brutal brother, Kurt, should be out of jail by now and living in the attic room again of apartment building 1. I wonder if Emile and Sylvie speak. Any sight of Isabella and/or Jean-Luc must send LaGrange into a jealous rage. Emile, after all, did discover Isabella, and loved her first. I wonder if LaGrange is wooing Isabella once again, causing untold trouble. Jean-Luc has seemed oddly furtive in speaking of her. I can only hope between my two sweet friends, Jean-Luc and Isabella, nothing is amiss.

Ray Guild, my roguish acquaintance, is here again in Paris, according to Jean-Luc–because of *Vogue*. I am sure Ray is delighted to be near Ludwig Turner – Brit, my artist, - because I know he has a sizeable crush on Brit. But then I do too. It seems I have the upper hand. Brit loves women. (Ray loves men.) And Brit may well come to love me for real–or so he has indicated.

The night before he left New York City to return to Paris, Christmas Eve, we had dined at a French restaurant, *Sel et Poivre*, on Lexington Avenue. Walking back across town, we had stopped on Fifth Avenue to admire the Christmas tree ablaze with lights, set back over the ice rink at Rockefeller Plaza. Standing side by side, hand in hand, he had quickly turned me around to him and kissed me full out, deeply, deliciously and for many moments. I clung to him almost desperately, because it was hard to see with closed eyes and so lost in a sensory cloud.

"I think I am falling in love with you, Elizabeth." It was a statement, said breathlessly, with a catch in the throat, to which I was too speechless to reply.

I am here now, close to him. Tomorrow will come and go, all too quickly, but when tomorrow is in the here and now I will be prepared, alive with longing, and ready for love.

Yet, full of questions. I know so little of him, his past a mystery, covert and hidden, the truth perhaps a concealed weapon waiting in the shadows.

To risk love, I must be on guard, for when it comes to giving myself to a man I barely know, my heart could be broken, oh, so easily - into a thousand pieces.

# Chapter 2

❦

## Duke Davis

After drowning in sleep since the all night flight from New York and arriving yesterday, Friday morning, on Saturday at 9:30 AM I descend for breakfast in the salon of the hotel, eager for the *café au lait* and fresh–baked croissant, the sweet butter and preserves from Brittany, the yogurt and cheese; in other words, *le petit déjeuner chez* Hotel Marcel.

A young man stands before Jean-Luc at the front desk. He seems tentative as he asks for a room.

"For how long?" Jean-Luc says in English. The young man is African-American. He has a handsome face the color of milk chocolate, with a chiseled nose, full lips, and dark brown eyes.

"I am not sure," he replies. "Is that okay? Can I keep it kind of open-ended? I am looking for someone – a friend I am trying to reconnect with."

"Of course, of course," says Jean-Luc. "*Bien sûr,*" and he hands him the key to the room that happens to be next to mine on the fifth floor, with its own balcony. His is much smaller than mine, only room enough for a pair of feet – yet the Eiffel Tower smiles down upon both of our balconies with its protective presence.

In the salon, eating my crispy croissant with delight, I have been listening to this exchange, and after the young man departs around the corner to the *ascenseur*, with backpack strapped to his shoulders, and carrying what looks to be a violin case, Jean-Luc comes from behind his station and perches on the chair beside me.

"Duke Davis is his name," Jean-Luc tells me when I ask. "Seems like a nice enough young fellow. Wonder how he came to Hotel Marcel?"

"Well, why not," I respond. "The price is right and the location – exceptional. And the gentleman who owns it happens to be extremely *gentil*," at which Jean-Luc beams. "But why did you put him next to me?"

"Why not? You are both from the U.S. Besides, he asked to see the Eiffel Tower from his room."

And, of course, that he can.

As my first Saturday on this trip to Paris, I decide to get my hair done, in anticipation of seeing Brit – perhaps as early as tomorrow. I will call him again this evening – with trembling hands, I don't doubt.

Is Brit too good to be true, I wonder? Is there a woman in his life to whom he is attached, has been attached, or who plagues him emotionally? Is there room for me?

I am still lingering over my *café au lait*. With a shake of my head to erase such thoughts of Brit, I begin to enjoy the morning bustle in the lobby. A man arrives with fresh flowers for the vases in the salon. Brigitte, a young Scandinavian girl, has arrived at her Saturday post at the front desk. Monsieur Marcel is usually off, on the weekends. Although he lives above the *pharmacie* around the corner, he drops in if there is some urgency. Today I guess the 'emergency' was seeing me on my first morning.

Later, after going upstairs to refresh myself and make an immediate appointment with the hairdresser around the corner, I descend to the lobby to go to the hair salon, and as I do so, I see Jean-Luc enter the hotel hastily. He draws Isabella behind him by one hand, she, as breathlessly beautiful as I remember, lustrous black hair flying behind her. They both appear concerned.

"*Il est déjà ici?*" Jean-Luc asks Brigitte, brow frowning, voice raised.

"*Non. Non, Monsieur...pas encore.*"

He gazes at me as Isabella rushes over to embrace me and Jean-Luc joins us.

"Ah, Elizabeth...all is well with you?" she gushes.

"*Mais oui!* How could it not be, with the Eiffel Tower to guard me, and two such friends as you," I say with a smile. "But tell me, just who are you waiting for so urgently?"

A look passes between them. Then Jean-Luc turns to me, "René Poignal."

'The detective?"

"*Oui.*"

And at this moment, that very person hurries into the lobby, trench coat tightly belted, even though the May day is warm.

"Ah, there you are Jean-Luc! And Madame Elizabeth...here again? Excellent." Then seriously to my hotelier, he says, "Jean-Luc. *Il faut parler!*" And the two men disappear around the lobby desk and back to Lean-Luc's office.

"What's that all about?" I say to Isabella.

She merely shrugs. A mystery to explore! A crime to solve! A challenge for me to my curiosity!

Now I know I am really back in my small hotel!

*Bien sûr.*

# Chapter 3

⌒ ⊙⌒

## Brit's Marais

His studio/apartment is on a sidestreet, la rue de Chance, off La Place des Vosges. It is a two-story structure, next to a shop selling exquisite *faience* (earthenware) in sunshine yellow with gray enamel tracings. This pottery comes from Provence.

I arrive there, at his instigation, on this serene Sunday morning, dressed in light clothes with a white linen jacket. I tap on the door of #2 Bis, which Brit told me to do when I phoned him last evening, and, of course, he is right there behind it waiting for me. His look takes my breath away, dressed in jeans and a crisp blue shirt, with that beautiful pepper and salt head of hair, and a smile so warm, so welcoming.

Both of us are initially shy, as Brit shows me into the rather ancient, wooden salon, with an old empty grate on one wall, and paintings leaning against the others. It is not bright in here, but I can see and sense the riot of color on those abstract canvases.

Within minutes, whatever diffidence between us is cast off, along with my white jacket, and he presses me to him in a sweet embrace, his lips lusty against mine. This lasts a long moment, filling me with hope and desire.

He releases me and leads me up wooden stairs to the second floor of his narrow house. There is a huge window on the far side overlooking a surprising lawn and trees, accompanying a grand, stone villa.

The sunlight pours through the glass, in front of which his easel stands. Paint tubes and a multicolored palette, a can of turpentine, drop cloths with bright drops of paint, brushes in different sizes – all are strewn about in the bizarre order of the artist. In one corner of the room there is a narrow bed.

"This is my work space," he says ruefully. "I know it looks messy..."

"But no," I interrupt. "It looks...used...the space, I mean. And what wonderful light."

I walk over to the easel. On its shelf, a small, framed painting is resting. Curiously for Brit, the work is quite representational. A black and white terrier dog stands on cobblestones in front of a door to a stone house. There is a green chair in the right foreground on which cabbages are piled.

But most curious, the frame is painted too. Cobblestones continue on the pathway across the frame and out of the picture. Dappled green leaves continue the trees in the painting, their color overflowing the frame, extending the vision, the whole like a flower opening.

"Oh," I exclaim. "It is so...open...like a book where the words spill over the edge of the page into the world...into life."

He gives me a broad smile, nods his head, and pulls me to him, and just as he had done downstairs, and just as he had done on Fifth Avenue in New York last December in front of the Christmas tree at Rockefeller Center, he kisses me until all sight blurs, and I am engulfed in the taste of his mouth, the smell of his skin, the press of his body.

Although the narrow bed beckons, after a long sensuous

moment, he draws me downstairs to the darker salon below, as he whispers, "not here. Not now, my love, but soon…when all is right."

My artist. My Brit. He certainly knows how to raise the bar of delicious sexual anticipation.

And longing.

How, when and where has he learned this, I wonder? How easily he raises one's hopes. How stealthy his approach. Most important, with whom did he perfect his technique?

And where is she now?

# Chapter 4

❧

## The Photograph

Duke Davis has a secret, I discover. We stand side by side on our separate balconies, gazing up at the Eiffel Tower. I have in hand the binoculars Jean-Luc gave me last fall. "The better to spy on your neighbors," he had said with a laugh. Duke is almost as eager as I to observe the shenanigans in the apartments across the street.

"Who's that?" he asks, as Henriette appears in her attic window on this Monday morning, cigarette dangling and hair in the usual snood.

"She's the Frontenac's *femme de ménage*," I explain. "She lives up there, above their apartment. Henriette is their general factotum, overworked and in demand at their dinner parties."

"Do they often have dinner parties?" Duke inquires, interested.

"Yes, indeed. You will see."

"And look…that man walking the little white dog. My gosh! What a bruiser."

I laugh. "You can say that again. That he is. A real bruiser! Here, take a good look," and I pass my binoculars over to Duke. "Kurt belongs in the attic of apartment building 1, where the

LaGrange couple live. He's the wife's brother –- and a minor jailbird… the dog is hers, of course, but he gets the dog-duty…"

"He's been in jail?"

"Oh yes, and more than once. He loves to come to blows in bars and even at dinner tables. And then he is carted off to the nearest jailhouse and locked up for awhile. He has 'anger issues!'"

"And in the middle building. Who lives there?"

"Well, it used to be Sasha Goodwin, you know, the photographer? He now has a room here in the hotel. An English lady lives there now with her 11-year-old daughter Amelia. Sasha, after the fire…"

"Fire?"

"Yes. Six months ago. The wife, Sylvie LaGrange, the bruiser's sister, who lives in number 1 building, threw a small homemade Molotov cocktail into Sasha's darkroom – and started a fire in that very apartment."

"What? What? I'm confused…"

"I can't say I blame you," I say, smiling at Duke. "Kurt detests Sasha – I guess because Sasha took his picture for the book he just published called *Les faces de Paris*. Kurt walking the little white dog. I guess Kurt was humiliated – being such a macho brute – with that tiny little bit of fluff. Who knows?"

"It's pretty funny when you think of it." Duke is grinning.

"Anyway, they had a fight on the street – the police came… Sylvie never got over it and took her revenge on Sasha. She caused the fire…Anyway, the *pompiers* came at night, sirens screaming and people hanging out of windows watching."

"I'll just bet," Duke says laughing.

"The place has obviously been renovated. Of course, Sasha wasn't allowed to go back there anyway because it was illegal to have a business in a residential building in the first place. So that's why there's a new person occupying the apartment in building 2. This street is full of drama," I say with a smile.

"I would say so," Duke agrees.

"I'm off," I say to him. "Have a wonderful day in Paris." And he nods a goodbye.

I return to my bedroom, leaving him standing there on his own balcony, suddenly pensive and deep in reverie.

As I move around my small room, I keep an eye on this young man. There is something poignant, almost wistful about him. He has told me he is in Paris to find someone.

"A friend?" I asked.

"Not exactly," was his answer.

On this Monday morning in May, as I peer through the glass French doors to the balcony, I see my young friend pull a paper from his pocket. It is not in good repair, frayed around the edges. He gazes at it for a long time.

I realize he is looking at a picture, a photograph, I surmise. How mysterious. Can it be the picture of the person he seeks? Suddenly, he glances my way, sees me watching him, and quickly stuffs the paper into his pocket, then shuffles off the balcony to his room.

I am sorry I interrupted his moment with the picture, sorry that he noticed me, sorry he might wish me off as a friend. I would hate that for I quite like him.

Also I've got to admit, I am curious about his background and his aspirations.

Duke Davis is different. He has a mystique that I wish to discover.

And that mystique will lead to an extraordinary place, astonishing as it unfolds, and strangely enough very close at hand.

So many mysteries, with Duke and his quest, and certainly with the hasty appearance of the police detective, René Poignal, in the lobby two days ago and a private conference with Jean-Luc!

Now what could that be about? My curiosity is piqued.

Most of all, my hopes for Brit and myself are overwhelming. Yet with all my dreams of love, I am eager for answers, and oh so ready to broach the private questions that come first.

Just who is Ludwig Turner? What is he?

# Chapter 5

## Tuesday Morning

It is quite early, as I step out on my balcony to greet the new day, sun shining on rooftops, air smelling sweet because of last night's rain. I lean over the railing, in my terry robe, and beneath me on the street I see Kurt with Sylvie's small white dog going for their morning walk.

Seeing him for the first time this trip makes my blood run cold, but I hurry inside to dress quickly, for a reason I do not understand, and down I go to the lobby. Ignoring the breakfast temptations, I stand on the steps of the hotel, watching the street.

Why? To see how Kurt will react to seeing me again? Or to see how I will feel on gazing at that frightening face?

Duke Davis joins me there. He offers me an open bag of macaroons from *Le Nôtre*.

"Have one. They are so delicious."

"Thanks," I say with a smile. "How did you come by these?" I reach into the bag and select a caramel macaroon, light as a feather and crumbly delicious to the tongue.

"Monsieur Marcel gave me one yesterday. He gets bagsful all the time! He told me where to go...you know... about *Le Nôtre*.

The breakfasts are great here at the hotel – but this morning, I had a craving…" He pauses, munching away on a mint green confection. "Oh so good."

There we are, two together, on the steps of Hotel Marcel, watching the people as they go to work, or hurry home to breakfast with long *baguettes* under their arms. I, of course, am awaiting the return of my nemesis, Kurt, with his tiny canine companion, primarily to see his reaction on recognizing my presence on his street once again.

"It's nice today," Duke says, at which I nod in agreement, when suddenly, across the street, we see a young girl emerge from the entrance of apartment building 2. She stands there, uncertain, then stretches her arms in the air.

"Who's that?" I ask.

"I think she belongs to the English lady in the fourth floor duplex," Duke says. "At least that's what Monsieur Marcel told me. She's about 11 years old, I think …home schooled…"

"Has Jean-Luc met the mother?"

"I believe so. She came over one day with the little girl… Monsieur Marcel thought the child's name is Amelia… apparently the mother asked directions. She's English and doesn't know her way about Paris yet very well. He says she is an artist, taught classes in a private school somewhere in Britain."

"Oh, yes," I say. "Jean-Luc told me she took Sasha's old apartment on the fourth and fifth floors. Hmm. She must do pretty well with her paintings because a duplex such as that one does not come cheap."

On the other side of the street, I suddenly see Kurt with the dog, rounding the corner, coming from the direction of the Champ de Mars. As he does so, the young English girl sees the dog, and moves toward it with arms outstretched, Kurt scowling as he sees this intrusion approaching.

"Uh oh," I say. "Here comes trouble."

And both Duke and I rush between on-coming cars to reach the other side of the avenue just as Amelia reaches the little Shih Tzu dog and leans down to pet him.

Kurt sees me. He sees Duke as we move towards him. He is furious with the whole interference in his quiet dogwalk, and he is not about to let the young girl near the animal. Neither is Schnitzel. He is a growly little creature and nips at the outstretched hand.

Amelia recoils. "He bit me," she says, near tears, just as Duke nears her and says, "You should never put your hand out to a strange dog. He might think you're about to beat him."

Meanwhile, Kurt is glaring at me, glaring at Duke, glaring at Amelia. "Get away, girlie," he shouts. "Get away," and he drags the dog brutally by its leather leash into the entrance of apartment building 1.

"Are you okay?" Duke asks Amelia.

She nods, then looks curiously at Duke. "Why are you in Paris?" she asks, gazing at him up and down. Her tone is nasty.

"None of your business, Missy."

"I've never met a colored man before."

"And I've never met a lily white little girl like you before with your British accent and pale face."

"I don't have a pale face!"

"Yes you do...just as mine is dark, yours is the color of milk."

"Is not," and Amelia bursts into tears.

I am watching this exchange, relieved that Kurt, even though hostile to me, was distracted over the dog/girl/Duke encounter. Now I can see that Duke is contrite over upsetting Amelia because he offers her the open bag of macaroons in appeasement.

Hesitating, Amelia peers in to view the contents. Her face lights up, as she selects not one, but two of the fabulous cookies, one chocolate and one a raspberry color.

She looks up at Duke, and in a tentative but very proper voice, says, "Thank you."

"You're welcome," he responds with a smile.

This is perhaps how friends are made.

# Chapter 6

❦

## Jillian Spenser

As Duke and I turn to leave and cross over to Hotel Marcel, I glance back and see Amelia standing uncertainly on the pavement, looking after us wistfully.

"Are you okay?" I call to her. She nods.

I find it strange that a child this age is not in school, but at that moment a tall woman rushes from the entrance of apartment building 2.

"Amelia!" she exclaims, the sound of relief in her voice. "Why did you go out? I was looking all over the apartment for you. I was worried." She is clutching the child's hand.

"She's all right," I say, approaching the pair. "Hi, I'm Elizabeth. I'm from New York, staying across the street – and this is Duke Davis. He's staying at the Hotel Marcel also."

"Oh." The woman seems to retreat. "I am Jillian Spenser. We moved here recently... from England...the Liverpool area... I am renting in this building..." she says, glancing at the entrance.

"We just came across the street because we saw your little girl..."

"Amelia."

"Yes, Amelia," I say. " She was trying to play with a small dog, but the man who held the leash was very rude to her and …anyway, I think the dog might have bitten her finger."

"Oh, oh," responds the concerned mother. "Are you bitten? Did the dog hurt you?"

Amelia holds up her right thumb.

"Well, it doesn't look too bad…sort of pink… but honestly, I can hardly see it…" Then to Duke and me, she says, "I do appreciate your concern. Thank you," in very proper British tones.

We nod in acquiescence, turn and leave the scene. As we enter the Hotel, I cannot help but say to Duke, "I really find it extremely odd that a young girl is out playing on the street when everyone else her age, at this time of day, is sitting at a desk in school."

"Jean-Luc said that the mother told him that she was home schooling Amelia…whatever that means."

On entering the lobby, Jean-Luc comes to me from behind the check-in desk, draws me off to a corner of the lounge area and asks me to dine with him and Isabella that very evening. Of course I am delighted.

"You like Italian?"

"*Mais oui,* Monsieur. I love it."

"Okay. We'll collect you here around 7:00."

"Excellent!"

Perhaps I can find out tonight what René Pognal was all about on the day after I arrived.

Also, what the hell does home schooling mean in terms of the young Amelia? I never realized how inveterately curious a woman I have turned out to be.

But there it is. It's true.

# Chapter 7

## Home Schooling

As we walk down the avenue toward *di Felice*, the restaurant Jean-Luc has chosen for our dinner, I glance up at the fourth floor of apartment building 2, where the blinds are open, all is lighted inside, and presumably, Jillian and Amelia are having their supper.

Or is Jillian helping her daughter with homework that she herself has assigned?

As we walk, I discover that Amelia's 'home schooling' consists of accompanying her mother to various museums; The Louvre, The Picasso, The Modern up at the Trocadero, the *Musée Dorsay,* others.

"Apparently, Amelia brings a book on French History and a sketch pad herself. At whichever museum, she sits on a small stool, next to her mother's chair, as Jillian proceeds to copy a small masterpiece into a sketchbook of her own," Jean-Luc answers my question.

"That's home schooling?" I say in wonder.

"I guess so," interjects Isabella.

Over a grand array of delectable Italian spicy meats and pungent cheese, our first course, I continue to question.

"Have you ever seen Jillian's work?" I ask.

"I have," says Jean-Luc. "They have a… well…watery quality."

"Watery?" I say with a perplexed grin.

"I don't know how else to describe them."

"She invited us over to the apartment last Sunday, and it's true. Her watercolors are kind of gentle…pleasant…kind of *pas define…*" Isabella remarks.

"*Indefinite?*"

"Yes. Indefinite…like her personality…agreeable but without much conviction."

Our lasagna arrives, bubbling hot, rich with meat and sauce and *parmigiano* which we devour with gusto.

"What about the 'masterpieces' she copies in her sketchbook at a museum?" I ask after a long draft of *Chianti*.

"I didn't see any sign of those, did you Jean-Luc?" says Isabella.

He shakes his head. "No. There was nothing around the apartment that I could see – just her own paintings of bridges and a landscape or two…not portraits…"

"What I don't understand is why she would come to live in Paris – mid-year – with an 11-year-old – where neither mother nor daughter speak the language? She's divorced, isn't she?"

Jean-Luc says, "I believe so."

"Hmm. It just seems like it must have been a sudden decision… kind of abrupt…to leave her teaching job in England so suddenly… in the middle of the school year…don't you think?"

Over glasses of *Limoncello*, I notice that Jean-Luc gives Isabella a side-long glance. Now what does that mean? The heady, citrus liqueur, after two full bottles of wine, has made us all extremely relaxed.

"Hey, you two. What's up? What are you in cahoots about?" I ask with a smile. They grin back at me.

"Well, it's funny that you are bringing up the whole thing of

Jillian Spenser and Amelia ...because there is a mystery about them, *sans doute.*" Jean-Luc is shaking his head.

"I love a mystery," I say with glee.

"Well, you know René Poignal...the detective. He came over the other day. We had a discussion back in my office...about this very subject."

"The subject being Jillian and her circumstances?"

"Yes," he says. "Jillian Spenser. She did leave England in a hurry. René has been notified by the Interpol police in Liverpool..."

"Interpol?" I am astounded. Jillian? Little Amelia?

"Something about art fraud. That she is a master copyist. Seems incredible, no? She apparently has been involved with a number of unsavory characters."

"Good Lord! I guess there must be big money involved. I've wondered how the two of them could afford to live in that expensive duplex – once our Sasha's – across the street from Hotel Marcel!"

"It's still very early in the investigation," Jean-Luc continues. "René wants me to keep an eye out...for strange visitors to her duplex...for any signs of expenditures out of the ordinary..."

"Like what?"

"A new, grand automobile...expensive antiques...you know... consumer spending on a large scale."

"That's seems improbable...with someone so self-effacing as Jillian. It seems impossible"

"But Elizabeth, would it ever occur to you that she could possibly be sophisticated enough... to be involved with these illegal practices in the world of fine art?"

"No. Of course not. The idea she has such a fraudulent hidden agenda is mind-boggling."

"Her innocent, rather simple appearance...that's what makes for a master crook! No one would suspect. No one would believe it."

No one would, I agree. No one is aware, least of all her

daughter. Her illegality is completely hidden from view by the undistinguished face and a sweet smile. Jillian Spenser must sweep the real facts of her life into a secret trash bin which contains old regrets, lost love – and shame - which thought closes out the evening.

On the walk back to the hotel, I find it curious that Jean-Luc and Isabella are on either side of me, not walking arm-in-arm as they did last fall. They are not exactly cold to each other, but neither are they warm to each other's touch...at least, not the way they were.

What is it that I sense? And what is it I need to know? I care about these two, and I want so much for them to love each other bigtime. It was there once – only six months ago.

It surely can be here again. I hope.

# Chapter 8

## Duke's Confession

It is near 10:00 PM on this sultry Wednesday evening. I have returned to my fifth floor bedroom from dinner with Ray Guild, my *Vogue* editor/friend, where we had discussed Sasha and his latest venture. In addition to *Les Faces de Paris* and *The Faces of New York*, Sasha apparently is planning to put together a new book called *Les Façades de Paris*.

"*Façades?*" I had questioned.

"You know…like the Eiffel Tower from the top looking down where the people below seem like ants and a tiny dog looks up… The dog probably looks like the little white one that appears in the ads for Sasha's book, *Les Faces de Paris*. God, the posters for that are plastered all over every kiosk in Paris!"

"The little white dog? You mean Schnitzel?"

"I guess so. The dog on the leash with that creature…"

"Kurt?"

Ray had let out a howl of laughter. "Schnitzel, eh, perfect. Your friend, Kurt, must be wild with rage at the humiliation of him being tethered to that bit of white fluff. Pretty humiliating. God, what a mean looking Dude."

"He doesn't only look mean!"

"Also, Sasha mentioned taking a picture of the Arc de Triomphe at night, with the lighted arch where one sees a couple of lovers kissing...facades, yes, but always with people. You know Sasha..." Ray began to laugh, or more like giggle. "Ah Sasha. He is indeed the bird on Nellie's hat."

However, I am here now back in my bedroom. My bed looks inviting. I go to open the doors to my balcony and find Duke on his, his legs curled under him in the tiny space, the Eiffel Tower beaming down on him with translucent light.

Duke has a nearly empty bottle of red wine in one hand and a cigarette in the other. I can see through the dimness that his face is slack, the expression in his eyes turned inward.

I kneel beside him on my own balcony, with cigarette and lighter in one hand.

"Hi."

Duke looks at me. For a moment, it's as if he doesn't recognize this older woman bending toward him.

"Oh...oh," he says. "Oh, Elizabeth."

"Yes," I say. "It's me." I settle myself on the stone floor. I light a cigarette, take a long, slow puff. "How're you doing?"

"You really want to know?"

"Yeah. I do."

He is silent beside me. "You don't have to talk," I say, breaking the emptiness. "But sometimes it's best...you know, to vent."

He still doesn't speak.

"You know good old American me. I'm no gossip, nor am I a meddler. But I am your friend."

Duke emits a long sigh. In a soft voice, almost inaudible, he utters "I could use a friend right now. I could sure use a friend."

I wait a beat. "Well, Duke, you got one."

With that he shifts position, sitting up straight. "It's really tougher than I thought it would be. I don't know how to approach him."

"Is this the person you came to Paris to contact?" I ask as gently as possible.

"Yes…not exactly a person I know…more like a relative I don't know. I looked and looked." Duke's mouth is trembling. "My momma gave me some clues…she even gave me an old photograph of him that she had from 20 years ago…and, well, I guess I know where he is…at least I think it's him."

"You've seen him?"

"I'm not sure. But – well – I'm almost sure…" He stubs out his cigarette angrily. "It makes me so mad not to know what to say to him – if it is he – do I just announce myself? Do I say do you remember when? Do you know that I exist? And now that you do, what are you going to do about it?" Duke takes a long, final swig from the bottle.

I am mesmerized by this monologue and deeply curious. "What kind of relative?" I question, although I think I already know what his answer will be.

Again there is silence.

"Is it an uncle? Maybe your momma's brother?"

"No."

"Is it a cousin?" Duke shakes his head.

Now I am speechless, waiting quietly, puffing away, until he finally blurts out, "My father."

I look at him and see that tears are slowly rolling down each cheek.

"Oh Duke, my dear. How hard for you. Your father. And he doesn't know about you? I wish I could help in some way…but this is your dilemma and no one but you can resolve it." I reach to touch his hand. He pulls away.

"I know. Nobody but me can help me face this. Momma

tried – but even she didn't have much hope for him recognizing me. She was always against my even trying to find him – but I have to. I have to know what I came from. I have to know for ME...so I can begin to know who I am," and the tears really start to roll.

I know it is partly the wine – a whole bottle – but also the pain Duke is experiencing is real and deep. Now he allows me to touch his hand.

"Do you know where he is in Paris? Have you found out yet where he lives?"

"I think so. I really think so," he mumbles.

"Would you like me to go with you there...not to be with you at the moment of seeing him – but just be there waiting downstairs... kind of moral support?"

Duke looks at me startled. "You'd do that for me?"

"Of course. What are friends for, " I say, smiling at the *cliché*.

"He's not far, you know. In fact, he's right here."

"What do you mean?" It is I who am now startled.

"Across the street."

"No!"

"Yes. He lives in that 3rd apartment building...the man who you say is always giving dinner parties. It's him. I am sure of it."

And Duke proceeds to tell me the story of long ago and his conception – as he heard it at his mother's knee.

Pierre Frontenac, a man with a secret no one could have imagined.

# Chapter 9

❧

## Blues in the Night

"My momma told me," Duke begins.

"When you were in knee pants," I counter, recalling the famous soul song. "My momma done tole me, son." I say grinning at him

"A man is a two-faced, he gives you the glad eye,
And when the sweet talk is done," Duke returns.

"A worriesome thing, he leaves you to sing,
The blues in the night," I finish in my most dulcet soprano.

We both burst out laughing. When that subsides, I say, "I know it's not so funny, Duke, what you are going through, but I promise you, your quest is the right one."

"I know it," he says "What is the best way..."

"To approach him?"

"Yeah. I don't know how."

"Well... I have met Monsieur Frontenac. In fact, I've been at dinner in the apartment..."

"You have?" he says, eyes lighting up. "What's he like?"

"That I don't know, Duke. He is not very forthcoming. But how, possibly could he have come to know your mother?"

"She said he really loved jazz and would come to the club where she was singing – 'course this was 20 years ago…I doubt the club is still there…"

And Duke proceeds to tell me what she told her young son about her affair with his father.

"She only told me a couple of years ago…when I began to ask… she told me she had an old picture but she never let me see it."

"I thought she gave it to you. How did you come by it?"

"I stole it from the drawer in the little table by her bed," Duke says, hanging his head. "I know I shouldn't have." He pulls the photo from his back pocket and hands it to me.

The picture is blurred, the image shadowy, but it *has* been 20 years since it was taken, after all. A man is lying on a divan. There are careless mounds of lady's clothing surrounding him – silk slips and lace panties, black stockings, and a garter belt he holds in one hand.

The shirt collar is open at the throat. His trousers are black, legs spread apart, one knee raised, and he wears a languid smile on his face.

"It's all I have to go on …this picture…all I have of my father… except his name."

"His name?"

"My momma named me Duke…after Duke Ellington. She gave me the last name of Davis, after Miles Davis. She named me after people whose music she loved. But I have a middle name. Pierre."

I cannot help but gasp.

Duke pauses. "She never married …oh, there were men…" His voice drifts off.

"Where is your momma now?"

"She died of diabetes…two years ago…"

"Oh, Duke. I am so sorry."

"I've been living with her sister and her husband." Duke hesitates. "He's white."

He waits for that fact to register with me. I say nothing.

"Since high school, I've been playing bass in a Chicago club called The Round House...I'm pretty good – make an OK living..."

"I'm sure she'd be proud of that."

He nods in agreement. "I also play the violin."

"Really. Classical?"

"Yeah, but mostly jazz violin."

"I don't think I've ever listened to a violin in jazz."

"It's great! So much flexibility...complexity...It goes over really well..."

We are on our separate balconies, communing together. He rises. "I think I'll take a little lie-down," he announces softly. "I'm really tired."

"Of course. Me too," I say, getting to my feet. "It's been a long day." I return to the haven of my room. And what a day, I think.

But not nearly as long a day as it will be for Monsieur Pierre Frontenac when he meets the dark skinned young man named Duke Pierre Davis.

Without Pierre Frontenac young Duke Pierre Davis is an orphan. Just how will that bourgeois gentleman react to probably the only child he ever fathered in his lifetime. And a son of a different color, at that.

# *Chapter 10*

❦

## Pierre Frontenac

Pierre Frontenac. How extraordinary. With his up-tight persona, I would never suspect he loved jazz. 20 years ago, although married to Elise, he apparently managed, on occasion, to frequent a *boïte* near the Boulevard Raspail, featuring a gorgeous, black American singer named Suzelle. She was a Billie Holiday clone, sultry, languorous and sleepy.

The place was called simply *Le Club*, according to Duke. Its patrons were jazz lovers, and they were devoted as well to the zinc bar, the tiny dance floor (although most came just to listen), and an American quartet made up of young black men.

Duke had described how Pierre Frontenac became obsessed with his momma, Suzelle, how at first, the Frenchman had merely stared. Suzelle was aware of his interest and played to him in her soul songs of love, moving close, directing the sensuous words to him personally. Finally, undone, he had rapaciously bedded her on a couch in her shabby dressing room, amid skirts and bustiers and silk net stockings.

"It became a habit for over a year, momma told me, until she returned to the States. Back to Chicago," Duke said.

I am sure Pierre Frontenac was never the same. Nor would he have had another such liaison where his head was completely obliterated by lust. He was just not the type.

This is part of the story that Duke related to me earlier, on the balcony of Hotel Marcel on this sultry night in May, a story that started in a jazz club. I know that Frontenac loves the sound of music – after all, delicious melodies always emanate from each and every dinner party – but jazz and Suzelle – these are revelations.

"Momma told me he couldn't get over how he'd yell out when they made love...he was so proud of himself...I guess," Duke had revealed.

"I'm sure," I had said ironically.

It was extremely difficult for me to imagine that repressed little man *in flagrante*, but the evidence of his passion was sitting right next to me, perched over the avenue below, staring into the Frontenac apartment.

"We have to get you over there." I had said.

"The sooner the better. Then I can go home."

"You may not want to," I remember saying, touching his face. "You may not want to at all."

# Chapter 11

࿊ ꙮ ࿊

## Confrontation

Duke and I had agreed last night to meet on our balconies at 8:00 AM this Thursday morning to case the Fontenac apartment.

We are here now. It's a cloudy sky, awaiting the patter of rain, as we peer across the avenue. And, *voila,* the face of Henriette appears in the attic window, with the usual cigarette dangling from her lips. She disappears for several moments, then we see her downstairs in the dining room, bustling about the dining table, setting out two large coffee cups and a basket of rolls for the Frontenac breakfast. The table is set with a place at each end, with a long flat expanse between the two potential breakfasters.

He comes into the room first, *Le Monde* rolled up in one hand, as Henriette approaches with a coffee maker and pitcher of warm milk. Pierre Frontenac merely bows *bonne journée* to his *femme de ménage*, but it is obvious that he does not speak.

"He's there, all right," I say to Duke who is mesmerized by the scene, totally enrapt.

"My thought is that I go over and tap on the front door and ask Henriette if I may speak to Monsieur. You can be waiting with me, out of sight in the hall, and when he comes to the door…"

"What will you say," Duke says, turning to me anxiously.

"Well, first I'll say hello and ask him if he remembers me from the dinner party – he will, I know, because I was the one who fingered Kurt Vronsky last fall, in that very apartment...by the way, I saved Frontenac money too, I believe –"

"Yes, yes, but what then? What about me?"

"I will ask to enter and tell him I have something most important to discuss with him. I wouldn't be surprised if he asks me to join him for coffee."

"And then?"

"Henriette will bring another cup and when we sit down, I will say that I have someone surprising that I think he should meet."

"Just like that?"

"Why not? At least I can try."

And so it comes to pass that Duke and I, under one of the Hotel Marcel's large umbrellas, because it has started to drizzle, cross through the traffic, go up in the elevator to the fifth floor in apartment building 3, and approach the Frontenac door.

Henriette does appear when I tap. I speak my piece, and indeed Monsieur comes forward, quite cordially (for him) and leads me inside to the salon and dining table.

Duke is outside the closed apartment door in the hall, dripping umbrella in hand. If a dark-faced man's face can turn pale, his does.

Before Pierre Frontenac and I have the chance to really get down to brass tacks, other than minor amenities, Elise Frontenac appears in a nightrobe made of dark blue silk.

The lady of the house looks totally surprised, mouth open in a half smile, to see an unbidden guest at her table, and of course, I am completely taken aback. I had not anticipated a third party at the start of this moment of truth.

Whew. It's getting *compliqué!*

How am I going to separate these two? It is only fair to Duke and Pierre Frontenac to meet together alone. A wife, ignorant of even the idea of a Suzelle, much less of an illegitimate black son, well, the truth might be enough to cause an incredibly hysterical scene.

I had noticed in the past Elise Frontenac's tears and her emotional fragility and realized the encounter with Duke might really put her over the edge.

In a tremulous voice, after a sip of *café au lait,* I ask Monsieur Frontenac if he might come over to the hotel, later in the day, at his convenience, of course, and meet the 'surprising someone' I am sure he will find important to him.

My host harrumphs for a moment, then glancing at his wife, not quite knowing how to respond, he finally agrees to stop by around noon before his business luncheon on the Right Bank at 1:00.

It is settled. I thank them both and hastily make for the front door.

"No, no, don't get up. I will find my way out, and thank you for the coffee – and for listening to me. Bye, bye," and I am off.

Duke is leaning against the wall, washed-out looking and nervous.

"Monsieur has agreed to meet you later at the hotel – around noon."

"He knows it's me?"

"No, no, of course not...just someone surprising he should know..." I feel somewhat deflated, but at the same time victorious because there will be a meeting.

"Mission accomplished," I say, grabbing Duke's hand, pulling him toward the elevator, leaving behind a small puddle on the floor of the hall from the dripping umbrella.

*À midi.* When it will all hang out.

# Chapter 12

## The Office

On our return to Hotel Marcel from across the street, I take Duke back to Jean-Luc's office. The door is open, and our hotelier is writing in an account book open on the crowded desk behind which he is sitting.

"Eh, come in, you two. Come in," he says, rising, beckoning to us as we pause at the entrance of his miserably cluttered workplace.

Duke and I stand there, quite without words, until Jean-Luc asks, "Well, what is it? What can I do for you? You both look…"

"I know, I know," I say hurriedly. "It's…well…it's a situation that has come up…and I was wondering if it is possible for Duke, here, to use your room?" I gesture with my hand about the small place. "Only for a few minutes…"

"What do you mean 'use my room?'"

"Well," I say, as Duke shifts uneasily from one foot to another. "It's that Duke has an appointment at 12 noon today…and it should be private…not out in the salon or lounge where it might be crowded with people…I mean his conversation will be a sensitive one…"

"Now, wait a minute…" Jean-Luc looks puzzled. "You want

to have a private conversation in my office with someone at noon, Duke? Is that right?"

Duke nods. He looks helpless, hands hanging at his sides. "Yes, Sir. If it is possible, Sir."

"Oh, stop calling me Sir. Call me Jean-Luc."

"Jean-Luc," the young man says, smiling for the first time in hours.

"*Bien sûr,*" Jean-Luc replies, returning the smile. "How long do you think you might be...with this conversation?"

"I'm not sure...but it shouldn't take forever..."

"No, of course it won't," I interject. "You're sure you don't mind?"

"*Non.* It's okay. Sorry it's so messy. But there are two chairs at least – here, behind the desk, and the one next to where you are standing, Madame," and he smiles again, closing the account book.

"Thank you, Monsieur...*Merci,* Jean-Luc." This time Duke is beaming.

"Look, it's only 10 o'clock now, so we'll get out of your hair..." I say. "Be back about five minutes before noon."

"May I ask who the person is...?"

"You'll see, you'll see," I interrupt, taking Duke's hand and once again dragging him from the scene.

We sit in the lounge area, the two of us, leafing through the newspapers and magazines, even old guidebooks, anything to pass the time. We do not speak. What is there to say? Jean-Luc appears around 11:30, takes up his station behind the entrance counter. He waves at us, picks up the telephone, and talks rapidly to a contractor on the other end about repairs to the *ascenseur* which are a constant bother.

It is now almost 12:15. Suddenly, we can see through the front lobby glass door the figure of Pierre Frontenac as he approaches the hotel. He wears a proper gray suit and carries a small wrapped up umbrella and a brown briefcase.

As he enters, Jean-Luc rises to his feet.

"*Bonjour,* Monsieur Frontenac. Ça va?"

"*Oui,* Monsieur Marcel, *et merci.*" He glances over to the lounge, sees me sitting there, and comes forward to shake my hand.

"Ah, Madame," and he bows slightly as a frown spreads across his brow.

"Thank you for coming, Monsieur Frontenac," I say. "We really appreciate it." Turning to Duke, then back to Pierre Frontenac, I continue, "And this is Duke Davis, the person I mentioned this morning. If you would follow me," and I imperiously move through the lobby and around the front desk toward the back office.

I notice Jean-Luc's face. His jaw has dropped and his eyebrows are in quizzical arcs.

Pierre Frontenac looks nonplussed, but he seems agreeable enough as he follows me into Jean-Luc's office. Duke goes behind the desk and stands next to the chair. (Good move, I think. Gives him a position of some authority.)

Turning to Duke's guest I say abruptly, "Now I will leave you two alone," and I quickly close the door behind me as I exit.

I have decided to return to the lounge area and continue leafing thoughtlessly through the familiar magazines and booklets lying carelessly about on the coffee table in front of the sofa.

Only moments pass, when suddenly I see a frantic looking Pierre Frontenac, clutching his briefcase and small umbrella to his chest, rush from the rear of the building and straight out the front entrance to the hotel. His eyes are popping from his head and his eyebrows seem to reach his hairline.

"*Mon Dieu,*" whispers Jean-Luc, rising to his feet, as I rush to the rear and through the open door of Jean-Luc's office.

It is empty.

Of course.

I find Duke on his balcony upstairs on the fifth floor. He is sitting forlornly on the stone floor. "I showed him the photograph. He just freaked," Duke wails.

"Did you say who you were...that you are his son?"

"I mentioned my momma's name....you know, Suzelle...and he freaked even harder."

"But did you say you are his flesh and blood...that, that you are his son?"

"Not exactly."

"Oh, God, Duke. I'm afraid this is not good," and I plop down beside him on the cold stone

# Chapter 13

❦

## Truth

It's Friday. This morning Jean-Luc calls from the front desk. It is 8:30 AM.

"Pierre Frontenac is waiting downstairs and wishes to see you. By the way, do you have an appointment with Madame?" I hear him question the guest in front of him, half off the phone.

"It's OK, Jean-Luc. It's OK. Just tell him I'll be down in a minute – and you might give him a coffee or something."

I quickly finish dressing. I have no idea what to expect from Pierre Frontenac and his obvious panic from yesterday.

What? Wrath? An emotional outburst? Disgust?

What awaits me is totally unanticipated.

"How much?" are his first words to me as I descend from the *ascenseur* and stand before him in the small, empty hall next to Jean-Luc's office.

"What do you mean, 'How much?' How much what?"

"Madame, that's what this is all about, no? That photograph! Money. Blackmail!" he says angrily, twisting two fingers together in an obscene gesture. "Nothing but money, money, money! That's what you Americans are all about!"

Monsieur Frontenac has turned red. I look at him with a mixture of anger and pity. Poor man is SO oblivious to reality.

"*Non, non,* Monsieur. You do not understand. This is not about money, I can assure you," I respond. And suddenly, I am just as angry as he.

"No sir. This has absolutely nothing to do with the good old American dollar! This is about patrimony. Patrimony, Monsieur Frontenac!" My eyes are blazing.

There is a dead silence. Pierre Frontenac is stopped cold. He seems to be trying to process this thought. Patrimony. His lips working, his eyebrows in a question mark, Pierre Frontenac is slowly absorbing the mind-boggling thought.

"Patrimony? Patrimony?" he repeats softly.

Equally softly, I say, "Monsieur Frontenac, Duke Davis is your son."

His face changes before me, eyes beseeching.

"My son," he whispers. "A son?"

What? Understanding of my words? Understanding of his past, his lust? His love, this childless man. A black son?.. no, no, half-black?

And then the thought of childless Elise...his wife...and of Suzelle, and the grand, sexual passion that had so consumed him 20 years ago, the past rising up before him in the form of a tall, handsome young man with dark skin.

I can see these thoughts in his beseeching eyes, and I know, for Pierre Frontenac, his world has changed forever.

And in a split second.

Never to be the same.

And in those eyes, I see the enormous perplexing question, what am I to do with him? With Duke? With the secret son I never knew existed?

"Ah, Lord, please tell me what am I to do," he whispers.

But it is not for God to answer.

It's entirely up to Pierre Frontenac, and somehow, he knows it.

# Chapter 14

‿◦჻◦‿

## A Picnic on the Seine

Saturday. Clear blue skies. The Seine at my feet. And Brit beside me.

We are sitting on the embankment made of raw stones, next to the Pont Neuf, the old bridge arcing over the river. It is warm in the sun. Brit has brought with him a small blanket, a cold hamper for a bottle of *Sauvignon Blanc*, with two wine glasses, and a large *tranche de paté de campagne*.

I am contributing a crusty, *baguette,* a wedge of *Brie* cheese, and a strawberry tart from *Le Nôtre,* plus, of course, a small bag of macaroons. (After all, they are the symbol of love for some of us.) And the Hotel Marcel has supplied me with the utensils, a couple of small plates, and several large checkered napkins in blue and white.

I wear fawn colored slacks, a pink shirt and white cardigan. Brit is in the usual dark jeans and, this day, a gray sweater that matches his eyes, and what eyes he has! It seems easy between us, although there is the constant current of attraction that is palpable to me.

He decides to spread the blanket for our picnic as I bring out the utensils, napkins and our comestibles, each carefully wrapped in wax paper, and the delicious loaf of bread.

Conversation is casual, with comments on the river traffic,

the acknowledgement of a couple of stray dogs who pass us purposefully, not nosing our food, and we share a laugh or two over the antics of Ray Guild who, Brit says, "Is determined to make me some sort of *Vogue* creation, which is not my style."

"He has a crush on you."

"You think?" Brit looks surprised, as he pours the wine and hands me a glass. "Hah. That's pretty funny. He may have a crush on me…but I have a major crush on you." He glances at me slyly.

"You do?" I say, blushing.

"Now, don't be coy, Elizabeth. You know I do."

"I don't know why," I venture. "Why me?…when you can be with any of the young whomevers you come in contact with."

"Now you ARE being coy. It doesn't become you."

"I'm not being coy. I'm serious. There are such temptations here in Paris… beautiful women on every street corner under the lamplight…"

"Hey, I'm not into that…" he laughs.

"You know what I mean. Why me?" and I turn to him directly. We are face to face.

There is a long pause. "Well, frankly, I am enchanted because you are a woman full-grown – because you are interesting and you amuse me and make me laugh. You are not some…arm candy," he says derisively.

At that I have to laugh. "Hardly!" I compose myself, "I know so little about you. How long you have been here in Paris? Have you ever been married? Children?"

"God no. I had a vasectomy."

I pause, startled. "Was there a particular reason?"

"I didn't want children," he says, taking a long sip of wine.

"Why?"

"Well, I'm an only child. I was close to my father – he died several years ago in a plane crash, and my mother… well…she was a different story. She has never approved of me...being an artist..." Then, more brightly, he pronounces, "My pictures are my children. I really do think of them that way. My legacy. Anyway, enough about me," and he turns away taking my hand.

I am fascinated with the issue of his secrets – his need to keep them. How he reveals himself to me – or does not reveal himself to me at all – makes me desperate to know more.

We break apart the bread. We spread the cheese and the *paté*. We open a second bottle of wine. We are talking and laughing and relishing being together.

But I cannot help myself. "And women?" I ask pointedly, suddenly.

"What?" He looks puzzled. "What's that got to do with anything?"

"Women – the history of your women...they are what shaped you, in a way...aren't they?" I say rather helplessly.

"That's utter nonsense. Look." And he puts down his glass and takes me by the arm. "I want you, want to hold you, want to make love to you, and you know why?"

My face is turned up to his.

"Because you arouse me when you smile – because your face holds depth and the lines of experience only make you more beautiful."

These words are nectar to my ears – and heart.

"Who can explain why one loves another?" he continues. "Who can explain the endorphins and euphoria that are elicited from one person and not another? Who can dissect love? And who is crazy enough to even try?"

His hands are holding my two shoulders.

"Elizabeth, don't dissect what is going on between us. Don't try. Please. Just BE. Just BE with me."

And I am once again lost in a kiss.

As I emerge from my sensuous haze, I murmur, "Ah, Brit. What honeyed words you speak."

He rears back, abruptly. "These are not just words! I mean them." His tone is strong, almost angry.

"You are still so…unknown to me…so unexplained…so hidden…"

"Look," he says. "I have tried to be honest with you. Come with me. Come back to my place – it's a small bed but we don't need king size…" He is looking at me imploringly.

I shake my head. "No."

"Elizabeth…"

"No."

"I want to make love to you."

I disentangle myself from his embrace and rise to my feet. "You told me once 'it should be when it's right'. And somehow, it's not."

"Why not?"

"I don't know."

And in truth I don't. But I feel disgruntled, out of sorts. Something seems wrong. I don't know why.

We collect our belongings in silence, mount stairs to the street, climb into his old Peugeot with its bucket seats, and drive swiftly through the traffic to Hotel Marcel. Not a word is spoken.

I leave him at the curb with a timid smile to which he does not respond, and enter the lobby devastated. What is the matter with me? Isn't loving Brit exactly what I want?

I am close to tears as I rise in the *ascenseur,* and when I arrive in my room the floodgates burst.

What is it? Why am I reluctant? I feel, in Brit, there is a private place, hidden away. Until he lets me in, fulfillment is just not an option. I remain alone.

And lonely.

But I will know when it is right. I will know, if only he is still there for me.

# Chapter 15

❧

## The Man Who Looks Like Ugarte

And he does! He is a dead ringer for Peter Lorre playing the devious crook, Ugarte, in the brilliant film, *Casablanca*.

It is Sunday, midday, and I am looking across the treetops to the other side of the avenue, in pensive thought, deeply sad about Brit who I have not heard from. Yet, I really haven't expected him to call. I know he has felt rebuffed and tell me, what man likes that?

However, now, I am distracted by seeing an unsavory looking character arrive on Jillian's fourth floor with a large package, wrapped in brown paper, which he places at her feet. I run to get the binoculars.

The blinds to her window are up, the glass panes open to the May air and sunlight, and I can distinctly see the two converse, faces serious. She leans to pull the paper apart to see what is layered beneath it – and it is in layers – then moves away to a table, takes an envelope and presents it to the ugly little man before her.

Money has changed hands. I'd bet on it.

At this moment, Duke appears on the balcony next to mine. He seems tousled, sleepy, yet at the same time, there is a kind of elation, a brightness in his gaze.

"Have you heard from him," I ask eagerly. "Has Monsieur Frontenac contacted you?"

I have noticed that the Frontenac apartment blinds have been firmly closed of late, no charming *diners* in view. Even Henriette's head has not appeared in the attic window in the morning.

"You've heard nothing?"

"No... nothing. Not a word," he says sorrowfully. "But I do have a job."

"A job?"

"I needed the money so I went up to the Boulevard Raspail where *Le Club* used to be...you know...where momma used to sing...where it all happened... and by God, they remembered her... the old guy who owns the place...Monsieur Gide...and well, last night...being a Saturday...they let me sit in on bass and it was super cool...they really seemed to like me."

"Duke! That's thrilling. How brave of you and how great you were appreciated."

He is beaming from ear to ear.

"But isn't there already a bass player in the group? What about him?" I continue.

"He's pretty old. He even played with momma. I couldn't believe the place was still there. But the bass – a guy they call Hooch – he wants to retire anyway, so I'm to start Tuesday night and for a few weeks, Hooch and I will spell each other until he's ready to leave...wants to move south...that's southern France," he laughs.

"Fantastic," I say and we both turn to look across the street.

"Who the hell is that?" Duke says on spying 'Ugarte'. "He sure is ugly."

"*Bien sûr.*" And I tell him of the envelope that changed hands.

"What do you suppose is in that package?" Duke shakes his head.

"It looks like boards of different sizes, stacked together...I bet they are canvasses...you know, to paint on. How odd!"

"Why can't she just go to an art store?" Duke is still shaking his head.

"Perhaps because these are special canvasses," I say. "Maybe they are old, used, that she can strip down and paint over, giving the impression of...age...to the master forgeries she paints."

What do you know! Now, here is indeed a thought to pass on to René Poignal.

# Chapter 16

## The Phone Call

I hear the phone ringing and rush from the balcony to answer.

"I've been a real jerk, Elizabeth," are his first words.

"Me too," I say. "I'm sorry to…pry…"

"No, it's me. I know I'm…well… guarded. Somehow I can't help it…but, look, I'll tell you anything and everything you want to know about my past…there's not that much…God, I haven't slept all night…"

"Me too."

"I want to see you," he says, words crowding each other. "When and where doesn't matter but the sooner the better. I can't seem to work…and you know the show – my show – at *Fernand et Fils.* – is so soon… next week-end…but that's not the reason…I just want to see you…"

"Tomorrow night?"

"Yes, yes," he says, relief sounding in his voice. "I'll pick you up at 7:00."

"*À demain,* Brit."

"*À demain,* my dear."

I rest the receiver back in its cradle and roll back on the soft pillow as tears of relief fill my eyes. *Demain.*

# Chapter 17

## Apartment Building 2
## Fourth Floor

It is Monday morning. I am in the lobby of the Hotel Marcel, looking for Jean-Luc to report to him the sighting of the sinister visitor yesterday who came to Jillian Spenser's apartment with a large package. He – Jean-Luc – I know will convey this to René Poignal, and also that I believe the package contains old canvasses.

When, lo and behold, Jillian Spenser appears with Amelia! There is no one behind the front desk at the moment.

"Do you know where Monsieur Marcel is?" she asks me.

I shake my head.

"We were looking to speak with the young man, Duke."

The girl holds a pink piece of paper in her hand. On it, she has drawn the picture of a small, fluffy white dog. The little animal is on a leash held by the figure of an ape-like man, directly behind the Shih Tzu. The dog is snarling, teeth bared.

So is the man...snarling and with teeth bared.

The rendition Amelia holds is remarkably drawn.

"My," I say. "This is a terrific picture. It's for Duke?"

"Yes. It's a present. He gave me cookies. I give him this."

A fair exchange, I think.

"It seems you have inherited your mother's talent," I say, smiling at Jillian. "I really would love to see some of your work, one day, if you have the time. Jean-Luc and Isabella tell me your pictures are quite lovely."

The reserved British lady nods at me with the beginning of a smile. "Thank you. Yes, I can show you some work, if you like."

"I do 'like'," I say with a grin.

She doesn't grin back. I am not sure she knows how to grin.

We arrange a date for tomorrow afternoon. "Around five?" Jillian declares. "I will give you a spot of tea."

"How nice. If I should run into Duke – if you haven't found him – may I ask him to join us? I know he would love to have Amelia's picture."

"That would be fine," Jillian says, looking hastily about the lobby, then taking Amelia's hand and leaving. "Be sure to get off the elevator on the fourth floor," Jillian calls over her shoulder as she pushes through the lobby door to the street.

I nod. Aha, I think. I will have a chance to see if there are any mini-masterpieces in view. And I wonder what is on the fifth floor. Will she have an easel in front of the window there to catch the light, as Brit does on his second floor? If she does, I have yet to see it. The fifth floor blinds are always drawn.

Duke rounds the corner from the *ascenseur*.

"Hi there," I say. "Listen, the English lady and her daughter..."

"Amelia?"

"Yes, Jillian and Amelia were just here looking for you. They invited us both to tea at five o'clock tomorrow afternoon – partly to see some of Jillian's paintings – but also the little girl has something special for you." Duke's face lights up. "Can you come with me?"

"Why, yes," he responds quickly. "That would be nice. Real nice."

And so the stage is set.

# Chapter 18

❧

## Diamonds in the Rain

Brit arrives at 6:45 on Monday evening in the Peugeot. I am already waiting nervously in the lobby, dressed in the same little black dress I wore when we first had dinner last fall. He wears a jacket, this night. His handsome face looks strained, older than I have seen him, but still, oh so appealing, perhaps even more so, for it shows emotion.

He hugs me to him with a smile of relief, saying nothing, opening the car door for me, settling in beside me.

"I thought I'd take you to a fish place over in St. Germain. It's got superb seafood. You do like seafood, no?"

"I love seafood."

It has just started to drizzle as we wend our way toward the restaurant, called *La Fresca*, just off the Boulevard St. Germain, on a tiny street, almost an alley, called rue Homard.

"This is the fishmongers district...these particular streets," Brit says.

We both seem stiff, formal, constrained.

*La Fresca* is small, with perhaps eight tables. The tops are of bare wood, but the place is lit by candles and smells of the sea, briny, salty.

Brit orders for the two of us. *Moules* in a light wine sauce; a beautiful grilled sole for two with lemon and capers; a crisp *Zinfandel*, chilled, to drink. It is perfect.

And he starts to talk. But first to question.

"And what about you, Elizabeth?" His tone is soft.

"Me?"

"Yes. You. Your men. You wish to know of my women? Hah. That's rich. For me, there has really been only one that meant anything. But you? How much have you hidden? What have you withheld?"

"I never thought of it that way," I say ruefully.

"What you don't understand is that I couldn't care less about the other men in your life. They are irrelevant – and they are NOT 'what shaped you'! You are what shaped you – you alone."

"Maybe influenced me?" I say feebly.

"Darling, we all come with baggage. You know that. For me, I lived with a woman for several years. She died of cancer nine years ago. Is this what you want to know?"

"I am sorry Brit. So sorry."

"No. It's okay." He touches my hand. We are eating slowly, sipping slowly, food almost forgotten. "I loved her, yes. We never married...neither of us wanted that piece of paper. She was an artist – ceramics, small sculptures – she was my artist mate."

"What a lucky lady."

"We were both lucky. And I am luckier because I met you."

"Then I am luckiest still." We have both stopped eating the beautiful food.

"When I first saw you...from the moment I saw you...I sensed somehow you understood me...and my pictures. From the get-go you seemed to see what I see...but it wasn't just that...it's your scent, your smile, a radiance you project..." He stops.

And suddenly we are in the car driving rapidly back to Hotel Marcel. I enter the little *ascenseur*, as Brit climbs the circular stairs to the fifth floor. He is talking all the way up, telling me how life is a series of moments and this is one so special and on and on.

I finally say, as we both reach the floor to my room, "Oh, shut up, Brit. Just come with me."

My bed is made, pristine before us. I do not turn on the lights. Instead, through the open glass doors to the balcony, now speckled with rain, we see the Eiffel Tower, blinking at regular intervals, tiny streams of light that turn the raindrops to diamonds.

And we are on the bed, naked in each other's arms, with diamond light sprinkling our limbs, floating in our hair, and touching our lips.

Pure magic.

How immediate and urgent this coupling feels. At dinner, Brit had shown me his vulnerability. He had swept away my own past. Now, his desire for me overwhelms any reservations I may have had. Here we are, glistening in the diamond light, lost among the gleaming drops of reflected rain, in a moment completely right for love. Oh yes. Right as rain.

# Chapter 19

## And On the Fifth Floor?

It is Tuesday morning. I have been here in Paris for 10 days. I leave a week from this coming Sunday – in other words, I have only another 12 remaining to be with Brit, to be near him. That's all. The thought is crushing.

The magical rain has cleared. The sun shines through filtered clouds, as I stand on my balcony, head bemused with love. Brit left around 5:00 AM with a hurried kiss, now frantic to get to work, full of artistic energy.

"I have to capture this night," were his parting words, as he left the room, suddenly empty for lack of him.

This coming Friday is the preview – the *vernissage* – of his show at the *Fernand et Fils. Galerie*. It is opposite the *Elysée Palace* on the rue Faubourg St. Honoré. The Friday preview is by invitation only; gallery patrons, buyers, art critics, and friends of the establishment and of the artist.

Saturday and Sunday, the show will be open to the general public. There has been a good deal of publicity about the event, as Ludwig Turner – my Brit – has developed a sterling reputation over the past years. He is considered one of the primary forces in the new world of art.

Today, my distraction will be teatime with Duke, at Jillian (and Amelia) Spenser's apartment, on the fourth floor, as Jillian has stipulated. I wonder what is on floor number five. There, the shutters are always shut, closed to view. Hmm, I wonder why?

I notice from my vantage point over the treetops, that there is still no sign of the Frontenacs. Even Henriette's head, popping from her attic window for a draft of her first morning cigarette, has not been seen. And as far as the LaGrange *ménage* is concerned, that too is hidden away behind damask curtains, and silent. Kurt and the dog, Schnitzel, I have not seen walking lately, although, one would assume that surely there must have been such excursions.

I am restless, pace nervously, yet the thought of the diamond-studded, rainy night of love fills me with euphoria.

In the salon, over the *café au lait* and shards of *gruyère* I consume distractedly, I see Jean-Luc behind his desk, brisk and businesslike on this week-day morning. In due course, he comes to join me.

"You look especially well, *ce matin*," he says, plunking down on the seat across from me.

"Why thank you," I say, feeling the blush rise to my cheeks. "By the way. I want to tell you. Duke and I are going to tea at Jillian Spenser's apartment this afternoon."

"Excellent. Perhaps you will notice something unusual," he says with a conspiratorial smile.

I proceed to tell him of the sinister man who had appeared at her door, with a large package which I thought might contain used canvasses – "or maybe even older frames," and that I would keep my eyes open for any and all details. "I shall report everything to you – and of course you can relay whatever you wish to detective Poignal."

"Even more excellent," Jean-Luc says, patting my hand, moving away to answer the lobby desk phone.

I idle away the day in the neighborhood, making small purchases – a colorful notebook, two key chains, with small replicas of the Eiffel Tower that light up, (for younger members of the family,) a couple of Tee-shirts that have the face of Picasso smoking a cigarette on the front. I eat a light lunch – a ham omelet and salad at *La Terrasse,* impatiently waiting for teatime to arrive and all the while, dreaming wistfully of my lover.

At 4:45 PM, I tap on Duke's door and call to him that I will meet him downstairs in the lobby. I hear his muttered "Okay," and down I go. Shortly, he joins me and we make our way across the street and up in the elevator of apartment building 2, to the fourth floor and Jillian's apartment.

She is waiting for us. There is a small tea table set out with cups and sugar and cream and sliced lemons and tiny cakes. The kitchen is on the far wall, and a teakettle is busily heating up on one of the gas burners. It is all very inviting, and although our hostess is not exactly thrilled to see us, she is pleasant.

It is Amelia who greets us – particularly Duke – with real enthusiasm. She is holding the picture of the ape-man and dog on its pink paper in one hand. Standing in front of Duke, she shyly presents it to him, and he, effusively thanks her, telling her what a perfect picture of that moment in time she has made. He oohs and aahs over the drawing, much to Amelia's delight, and her mother's pleasure.

"I'm so glad you came," Amelia says to Duke.

"Me too," he replies, and from his back pocket he draws forth a tiny box with just four macaroons inside, each of a different color. Amelia is ecstatic.

There are chairs about the room which we pull up around the tea table, seat ourselves, as Jillian pours. There is no sign of the infamous package, dropped off by the Ugarte-type scoundrel, but on the interior wall, near a door, I see a wooden, triangular piece of furniture, holding a number of watercolor paintings.

"Are those your work?" I ask. There are no framed pictures on the walls.

"Yes, they are – watercolors. I will show you after tea."

"Wonderful," I say, gazing about. "You have an upstairs too, in the duplex, no?"

Jillian nods, non-committal.

"Is that your workroom? Do you do your painting there… upstairs?"

Duke is munching tea cakes, watching us both, his head swiveling from one to another, because, of course, he is in on the mystery of Jillian's illegal trade.

"No, I paint *en plein air* – outside. You will see."

"And upstairs…are the bedrooms…?"

"No, we sleep down here," Amelia interjects.

With that, Jillian rises. "Come let me show you the pictures."

As we move across the room, we pass a small side table on which I notice an exquisite small oil painting on a stand, with an elaborate frame, curlicued in gold, a natural setting for neo-classic works of art.

"Oh," I say, pausing before it. "How very beautiful."

"Yes, it is." For the first time, Jillian looks pleased. "It's a Corot. '*Nymphe en Rose.*'"

"My goodness. It is lovely. So reminiscent of Degas…in a way. Soft, subtle, dreamy..How did you come by it?"

"I inherited it, actually," Jillian says, without hesitation. "The young girl in the painting is the daughter of Guillaume Moreau, who married Leonard Saxon, a British man whose daughter married into the Spenser family. This Corot belonged to my father, and when he died, I was bequeathed this beautiful picture."

"It surely is exquisite," I say, wondering about the veracity of this tale, which seems truthful, if a bit glib, (or perhaps is just much rehearsed.)

"I am the poor relative," Jillian says primly.

And we move to the holder of her watercolors which indeed, I find 'watery' and undistinguished. Pictures of the Thames flowing under bridges; landscapes with a pond or two; a beach beside a very wet-looking ocean. She certainly loves water, I think, this 'poor relative' with a Corot worth a major fortune.

Not so 'poor' a relative, if Jillian should sell it. Not so poor at all.

# Chapter 20

## A Day of Secrets

It is late Wednesday morning. I am preparing to go to lunch with my great friend, Sue, the Marquise de Chevigny, now widowed, with whom I had grown up in New York City. I had hoped to see her sooner, but she had been bedded with fever for the last week. Finally, she is able to get into Paris from her château in Montoire, southwest of the capital. We are to lunch at *Caviar Kaspia*, our favorite place to eat briny delicacies, enjoy the intricacies of gossip, and most of all, be together as old and dear friends.

As I pick up my purse and key from the bed to go below, the phone rings.

Brit? I hope.

But no. It is, of all strange men, Monsieur Pierre Frontenac.

"Madame?"

"Yes, Monsieur Frontenac." I recognize the nasal voice.

"I must ask you," his words are subdued, "has Duke left Paris? Has he gone?"

"Oh, no," I say. "He is still very much here– and eager to see you."

"He is? Well...well...What should I do?" Frontenac's voice is now agitated. "I don't know how to handle this."

"You can handle it like a father!" I say vehemently.

"I don't know how to do that."

"You'd better learn. Listen, Monsieur. Duke's mother is dead. He has no one, really, except a sister somewhere in America married to a white man."

There is a pause as Frontenac processes this bit of information.

"By the way, Duke has a job."

"He has a job? What kind of job? Really? A job?"

"Your son is a talented bass player. He had the courage to go to *Le Club* – I believe you remember *Le Club* – where his mother used to sing," I say pointedly. "The place is still very much there up near Boulevard Raspail, after all these years – anyway, he has a job playing bass. They think he's great."

There is a long silence.

"Are you still there, Monsieur Frontenac?" I ask. I know he is because I can hear him breathing rapidly.

In a very small voice he says, "Will you take me there...to hear him...see him? I don't want to go alone. I would much appreciate your being with me. You have no idea how hard this is..."

"I think I do, Pierre – if I may call you that. And I would be glad to help in any way to reconcile this whole situation. I think you don't yet realize what a lovely young man is this Duke Pierre Davis. You haven't had the chance, but I believe he will make you proud."

"*Peut-être demain soir?*" this said hesitantly.

"That would be fine."

"*Merci*, Elizabeth. I will call first...around 9:00 PM?"

"*Bien. À demain*, Pierre."

"*À demain.*"

In passing through the lobby of the Hotel Marcel on my way to the nearest taxi stand, I wave to a distracted Jean-Luc at his post at the lobby desk. He is distant, scowling, but manages to give me a quick smile as I go by.

As I climb into a taxi, giving the driver the address of the restaurant, *"près de La Madeleine,"* I wonder, what's with him? Jean-Luc. I am bewildered at the unrest I sense between the two, he and Isabella. I know how much in love they were when I was here only last fall.

I am first upstairs in the quietude of the pale green ambiance of *Caviar Kaspia's* small dining room. The banquette is deep and comfortable and a waiting ice cold small carafe of vodka is in its tiny ice bucket on the table.

Sue arrives, flushed and lovely, chic in a dark, military style linen jacket. We hug, double-kiss, exclaim happily over each other, order baked potatoes topped with caviar (what else in this emporium of the ultimate sturgeon roe) and settle down to speak of our lives, an exchange of catching up phrases, talking over each other with such delight.

"And how is your small hotel?" she asks finally, breathless.

"Always so intriguing," I reply. And I tell her of the black son of a man across the street, of my worry about the love affair between Jean-Luc and Isabella, of the intended visit to *Le Club."* I can't seem to get the words out fast enough.

"And that awful man in the attic?"

"Who? Kurt? I have only seen him once when he had a fight with a little girl over a small, white dog."

"Good Lord, what a beast!" Sue says.

Then I proceed to tell her of Jillian Spenser, who has taken over Sasha's old apartment in building 2. The fact that Interpol has contacted the police in the form of René Poignal about the quiet English woman being an art forger, Sue finds astonishing. Then I speak to her of the beautiful Corot, *'Nymphe en Rose.'*

"Good heavens! What an amazing hotel is the Hotel Marcel. I never heard of so many mysteries," Sue says. "Hmm. But you know, Corot – Jean-Baptiste-Camille Corot – he was known mostly for his landscapes – except he did a lot of small neo-classical portraits of his 18th century neighbors and relatives. They say he was very easy to imitate. In fact, I remember – there was a showing of his work at the *Musée d'Orsay* recently – and apparently, there were thousands of Corot forgeries made during his lifetime."

"Really Sue, you are something else! I'm really impressed with your knowledge of art," I say with a grin.

"Well, I haven't been in France all these years for nothing!" Sue says with a deprecating smile. "By the way, if this Jillian person's Corot is really a fake, she'd better not try to sell it in Paris. The French police are very aware and vigilant about art fraud, particularly if it's a French painting in question. Better your friend Jillian peddle it in America or even England."

"My 'friend?' I wouldn't call her that. But, Sue, you are so smart my dear. What do you say, shall we order another carafe, just for old time's sake?"

"Why not?" Sue says, beaming. And we are off again, talking of the trials of parenthood and our old lives as wives, now widows. Ah, Sue. So much in common, in spite of the different paths on which fate has taken us, yet we are sisters under the skin still and always.

Just as the taxi taking me back to Hotel Marcel rounds the corner of the avenue, I see a Mini-Cooper automobile drive swiftly towards the cross street. I can see clearly the tall frame and gray-haired temples of Emile LaGrange – the first view of him since I have been in Paris this time – and next to him a young woman with dark hair.

Isabella! It is she. I am sure. The dark lustrous hair gives her away. What in God's name is she doing with her rejected lover in his car in the middle of the afternoon? What about Jean-Luc and their love-nest in his apartment over the *pharmacie* on the next avenue?

No, no, I think. Not Jean-Luc and Isabella broken apart. Please no. They seemed so good together and I am so fond of both.

Talk about mysteries! Just what the hell is going on?

# Chapter 21

❦

## More Secrets

It's Thursday morning. Tonight I am to go to *Le Club* accompanied by Monsieur Frontenac – Pierre – to see Duke Pierre Davis strum bass in the quartet playing there. Duke had told me he was spelling the bass man currently playing until his retirement on Tuesday and Thursday nights, so I knew he would be at his bass *ce soir*. I have not warned my young friend of our visit to be…don't want to spook him… but I am eager to see, hear, and feel Pierre's reaction to seeing, hearing, and feeling his son in full-out expression of his talent, and of his past.

Until that time, I am doubly excited about meeting Brit for "a quick little lunch," as he put it, "because I need badly to see your face," he had said. I am to join him at the *Fernand et Fils.Galerie*, on the Right Bank. Brit is in the throes of setting up his show there. The *vernissage*, the preview, is tomorrow night.

I am wearing a navy linen shift that looks great with the white jacket, and I also know I am glowing from inside, because I am to see Brit, a thought that brings me such joy.

As I leave the *ascenseur* on the ground floor, I notice that Jean-Luc's office door is ajar. I hear the haunting horn of a Miles

Davis solo playing softly. Gently, I push the door open, after a small knock.

He is sitting at his desk, a doleful expression in his eyes, but he beckons me in.

"Hi," I say.

"*Allo.*"

"You don't look so good."

"I'm not."

"Oh, Jean-Luc." I sink into the only other chair in his office next to his desk. "Can I help?"

"No one can."

"Not even Isabella?" I venture.

"Hah! Least of all Isabella."

"What's up, Jean-Luc?" I ask with a sigh.

"Damned if I know."

There is a long silence, only the wail of Miles Davis' cornet.

"It's LaGrange, isn't it?" I venture again.

"How do you know?" Jean-Luc looks startled. So I tell him of seeing her in that man's Mini-Cooper on the way home yesterday.

"*Quel bâtard!*" Jean-Luc slams shut the large account book on the desk in front of him. He turns off the cassette player.

"We know he's a bastard," I say, "but why was she with him? Why is he back in her life?"

"He has something on her. I'm convinced."

"What?"

"Not sure." He rises. "Something about her father, I think."

"She won't tell you?"

"Not yet. Look, I've got to go," he says as I get to my feet.

"Of course, of course. Sorry to have kept you."

"*Non, non.* It's always good to see you." And he ushers me to the door.

On my way to meet Brit, I mull over this conversation, as the taxi hurtles through traffic towards rue Faubourg St. Honoré. I am alarmed for my two friends but feel helpless. There is little I can do.

I'm here. There is the *Galerie*. As I enter, I am greeted by an elderly gentleman who introduces himself as Monsieur Fernand, saying "And you must be Madame Elizabeth, *non?*" He is extremely courtly, and behind him, I see the tall figure of Brit, who rushes towards me with a smile and a quick embrace.

Over Brit's shoulder, I can see on the far wall of the elegant room, a large abstract painting in white and gray and silver. It is brilliantly lit and is the centerpiece of the exhibition.

"Oh," I say, as I move around him, drawn toward this work of art.

"It's called *'Diamants en Pluie'* – 'Diamonds in the Rain,'" I hear him say softly. As I approach, the painting gets larger and larger. I see, in the white section at the top, tiny black lines, like filaments of wire. The reverse is true, halfway to the bottom of the piece, with white lines, intricate in the black paint. I can almost see – but not quite – a silver outline of two human bodies, intertwined, clasped together.

I am speechless, as tears come to my eyes.

I notice a small red sticker next to the painting – a sold sticker. "It's already sold?"

"No," Brit says. "I put that sticker there because it is not for sale. It is for me to keep. Mine. You and me and the Eiffel Tower," he says with a huge smile. "Come, let's go to lunch," and he grabs me by the hand.

In something of a daze, he takes me around the corner to a tiny street, only several feet in length, where an equally small eating place is located, called *Bistro d' à Côté*. We find a banquette and Brit orders *canard confit* for two with *sautéed* potatoes and a bottle of *Pinot Noir*. He is obviously a most popular client of the establishment for the owner sends over a dish of pungent Greek olives, '*pour l'artiste en résidence*' with a big smile from behind the zinc bar, followed by a plate of slices of spiced ham.

I have been silent, smiling all the while, happy to be in his presence, and quite overwhelmed by the beauty of that picture and what it means to both of us.

"I can hardly speak, Brit. That picture – '*Diamants...*' It's... breathtaking."

"My darling. It was very easy to paint. I felt all of it. That makes putting it down on canvas at a fast pace...I mean, it was almost like I <u>had</u> to get what I felt down..."

"Well, you did, Brit," and again, tears fill my eyes.

"I hate to be in a rush," he says as the food arrives, the duck crispy, the potatoes soaked with the juice of the bird, "but we still have much to do. Monsieur Fernand has been really wonderful to me – but I like to manage the placement of my pictures myself. I told you, they are my children. Not '*Diamants*' of course. That one is me – and you."

I am mum, I can only look at him.

"I have made a small version for you, Elizabeth. One you can take home with you. Oh, Christ, I wish you weren't going home ever again. You should stay here. Stay with me here in Paris."

"I can't. I have obligations." My heart is beating fast. "You made a '*Diamants*' for me?"

"Well, there were two of us there after all. But why must you go back to the States? You told me you are here only until the 22nd? That's leaves us only a week! If you can't stay, at least postpone your departure a little, please. I beg you," and his face is so imploring, and my heart is so involved, I tell him that I will extend my visit.

Brit is elated. "I'll give you the little painting after the show on Sunday night. We will have that evening all to ourselves – the pressure will be off me and if you stay longer, we can have many more such evenings."

And with that, we devour the food and drink the wine so happily that I think I may die of delight.

Then, I had to ruin the mood.

"Did you ever paint a little painting, a companion piece to a larger one, before, for a lady in your life?" I ask.

Brit stops eating. He looks at me. "Why do you ask that?"

"I was wondering."

"Well, stop wondering. What if I had? The fact is I never did. But what does it matter to you and me?" His tone is cold. I know he is angry.

"You're still so unknown to me," I say weakly.

"Oh, stop with the 'unknown.' I am just what you see sitting before you. I'm sorry if that's not enough." And he calls for the check, for *l'addition*.

Why did I blow it? Why did I blight the mood? Here he has given me the ultimate gift – a gift of his talent – the gift of himself – if only for a little while – and I continue to pick at his past like some buzzard looking for morsels. It's enough to make even me sick.

I do go back to the hotel. I do change my airplane ticket, adding an extra week to my time in Paris in the hope that Brit's feelings for me will overcome any disgust he has for my prying.

Oh why, oh why do I seem to shatter the best thing to come into my life in lo these many years?

I've been burned more than once. I've been tormented and tormenting more than once, but this time, this moment, I must trust my feelings and throw caution aside, like a dead black rose. Be there for me, Brit. Please.

# Chapter 22

*Le Club*

Antoine, the night man at the front desk, calls me at quarter to nine in the evening to tell me Monsieur Frontenac is in the lobby. I descend in the *ascenseur,* dressed in my basic black dress, with the white jacket over my arm.

Pierre greets me with a formal little bow, saying nothing, and we proceed to the nearby taxi stand. On the drive to Boulevard Raspail, he says little, merely commenting about the pleasant weather – it is a particularly lovely evening, the air fresh and cool.

At the corner of the Boulevard, the taxi stops, and Pierre leads me along a side street, to a set of steps leading down to the *boîte,* *Le Club.* The jazz cabaret is buried beneath the sidewalk and the adjoining building, on which there is a neon sign.

Simply, *Le Club.*

I hear the sound of bass, piano, drums and sax floating up to greet us as we move down. It is the blistering sound of jazz.

It is dark on the stairs, but the music floats up to meet us as we move slowly towards it. Pierre is reluctant in his steps, holding back, but as the tune changes from the basement below to a soulful song, "Someone to Watch Over Me," a woman's shrill but clear voice articulating the plea, he stops in his tracks.

We finally reach the dimly lit room. It is crowded, but we manage to slip behind a small table near the entrance. I see Duke standing tall beside his bass on the tiny stage at the far end of the room, his long fingers busy on the strings of the instrument. He does not see us, for the light from the proscenium is on his face, as well as on those of the other musicians and the singer. His chin is lifted and his eyes are deep into the song.

I look at Pierre. His skin is the color of ash, his visage closed, lips compressed. His eyes are on the son he never knew.

The mood changes in *Le Club*. Duke moves forward, leaning his bass against the back brick wall. He picks up from a chair, a violin, and comes to stand next to the singer. She is a slight black woman – American as are all the musicians – with a waif like quality.

Duke strikes a chord on the violin. The piano picks up the melody. The snare drum scratches underneath, and the woman's voice begins the lyric to the famous Billie Holiday song, "Strange Fruit."

> *"Southern trees bear a strange fruit,*
> *Blood on the leaves, blood at the root,*
> *Black bodies swingin' in the Southern breeze,*
> *Strange fruit hangin' from the poplar trees."*

Duke's violin is tremulous in sound, exquisitely graceful in its phrasing, totally mesmerizing in conjunction with the woman's voice and the backup of piano and snare.

As she ends the song with the words,

*"For the sun to rot and the trees to drop, Here is a strange and bitter crop."*

The whole audience – young and old – black and white – Asian and Hispanic – is silent for a long moment, then rises to its collective feet, clapping wildly, murmuring one to another.

I look at Pierre. Tears are running down each cheek as he reaches for his handkerchief.

A boy with a white cloth wrapped around his waist brings two glasses of red wine to the table which we had ordered before the song. I am glad for the distraction because there is an emotional quotient here that neither Pierre nor I could have anticipated. Suddenly, what it means to be a black American has impact for both of us. For me? A friend.

For Pierre? A son.

Finally, after a long sip of wine, I say, "Do you want to speak to him?"

"*Mais oui*. Of course," is the curt, controlled answer.

Duke has not yet spotted us. There is a break in the set of music. I see him lounging languidly against the back brick wall, speaking with the drummer, when he glances across the room and sees me in my white jacket, which I have about my shoulders against the air-conditioning. He smiles, then pauses, uncertain.

All of a sudden, he starts moving toward us. I brace myself for what is to come. I notice Pierre, who has not taken his eyes off Duke, tenses too. As Duke approaches our table, a determined, yet surprised, look on his face, I rise from my chair.

"Here, Duke, Please sit here. Excuse me. I'm off to the ladies room," and I quickly move around the young man as he stands in front of his father. Pierre is looking up at him, a strange, proud smile on his face. His eyes are wet.

In the ladies room, which is full of pushing females – pushing to get to the mirror, pushing to wash hands, pushing to reach the paper towel dispenser, I stay as long as I can. Then, quite overcome with the scent of a mixture of perfumes, I walk back through the club, around the small dance floor, and see the two men in earnest conversation. They are animated, engrossed.

I step to the entranceway and out onto the bottom step to the stairway up to the street. The air is sweet. I light the cigarette I just happened to have secreted in my purse, for just such an occasion.

Whew! Father and son. Strange fruit.

After giving them more time together, I finally return to the table near the entrance. At the moment, the two men, one so young, one so very middle-aged, are looking at each other, eyes fixed.

There seems to be no animosity between them. They appear to have come to an acceptance, one of the other. As Duke rises to let me sit down, I see Pierre give Duke a slow smile, and Duke in turn beams back (because when Duke smiles, he always beams.)

To me, he says, "Thank you, Elizabeth. I'll see you on the balcony." And to Pierre, "Goodnight,… Father." Pierre blanches, but nods his head in acknowledgement. Then I see him smile once more at Duke's retreating back, as he goes to the stage.

In the taxi returning to Hotel Marcel, we are far more relaxed than we were on our earlier journey to *Le Club*. Pierre rolls down the window and the night air refreshes us both.

As we near our destination, Pierre turns to me and says, "I am most…full of thanks, Madame Elizabeth. You give me a grand present this night. It is *un monde nouveau pour moi*…a new world where I have a son." I can see his eyes glisten in the light from the street. "*Merci, mille fois.*" He clears his throat.

"He certainly plays beautifully," I say, trying to ease his emotion. "You should be proud."

"I am. Oh yes, I am."

There is silence until I question him on an issue that sooner or later must be addressed.

"Have you spoken to your wife?"

His head whips around to look me in the eye. *"Non."*

It is a curt answer. But he composes himself, and after a moment says, "Of course, she will have to know. *Déjà*, she finds.... me... there is something on my mind. I will tell her. *Meme, peut-être ce soir..."*

"I wish you well," I say, getting out of the car. Pierre follows me, and at the curb, takes my hand and kisses it in the oldest of European courtesies.

*"Bon soir, Pierre, bon soir. Soyez bien."* And with that I leave him standing there in the street, as he looks up at the window of apartment building 3, fifth floor, where the drapes are drawn and no light shines.

# Chapter 23

❦

## LeVernissage

It is Friday. This evening is the preview of Ludwig Turner's exhibition at the *Fernand et Fils. Galerie*. I have not heard from my artist/lover in the last hours before the event and since our aborted lunch – aborted by my probing into his past.

Frankly, I am a nervous wreck about how Brit will receive me at this social function. He will be surrounded by buyers, critics, friends of his and the gallery's, by reporters and museum board members. Although the general public is not invited, the crowd will be even bigger on Saturday, May 16, tomorrow, at the grand opening, when he will be inundated by the curious as well as serious art enthusiasts.

Just where does that leave me? Will he still give me the smaller version of 'Diamonds in the Rain' he painted for me? More important, will he still love me?

I make a hair appointment. I go through everything in my limited wardrobe, to determine how to present myself this afternoon at 5:00 PM at the gallery. I finally decide on a white pants suit, well cut and simple that I will embellish with a plain gold chain and gold shell earrings. Having made that major decision, I head off to my hair appointment around the corner.

Even from the fifth floor, as I enter the *ascenseur,* I can hear the sound of two male voices raised in anger. As the little conveyance descends, the furious tones increase until, by the 2nd floor, they are loud enough for the whole hotel membership to hear.

This is so unlike the decorum presented in my modest hotel. I am astonished that Jean-Luc would allow this to happen, until I realize that one of the raised male voices is his own!

And then, of course, I realize the other is that of Emile LaGrange.

The dreadful sounds come from behind Jean-Luc's office door. I pause beside it, incurably curious and frozen to the spot.

I can glean from the torrent of French words, the gist of the argument. Argument? More like a battle royal!

"She owes me," from LaGrange.

"She owes you nothing," from Jean-Luc.

"Her father promised her to me – to take care of her."

"He promised her to you? As if she were made of wood like one of his antiques? Ha! Her father's dead, Monsieur. And Isabella is very much alive and she's with me."

"Perhaps no more," LaGrange spits out with a sneer in his voice. "How did you learn she and I have met?" he continues, insinuatingly.

"She told me."

"She did not. She's scared to." LaGrange sounds triumphant.

"But Kurt – that *bâtard* brother-in-law of yours – did! I saw him on the street and he came up to me right *en face* and said 'my sister's husband has been all over that girl of yours, Monsieur Marcel. I've seen them in his car. How's that for hot news.' He was almost drooling with delight, the little punk."

"Kurt? *Merde, alors!* He is nothing but trouble. He's vicious. I could kill him. He had no right to tell you – of all people. He knew it would bring about a fight."

"And he was right!" Jean-Luc says vehemently.

"He loves to provoke people. He even told my wife I had seen Isabella. She went after me with a *parapluie!*"

The picture of Sylvie LaGrange beating her husband with an umbrella makes me burst out laughing.

"He should be in jail," Jean-Luc is mumbling behind the office door.

"I've paid enough to keep him out –those damn judges – so greedy – Well, never again. Kurt can rot there."

Suddenly all is quiet.

Then, Jean-Luc speaks. There is menace in his voice. "You stay away from Isabella."

"Ha! Just make me."

"No. She will. Right now she is intimidated by you – you are playing on her guilt – but she will get rid of you once and for all."

"Don't count on it," LaGrange rejoins. "Yes, she thinks she is in debt to me – for bringing her to Paris – for her job at Yves St. Laurent. You don't know half her story. She has never told you of her real background, has she? I can see by your face she has not. Little do you know… And yes, she is grateful to me. And she should be. Ah yes, Monsieur," he continues, his tone full of innuendo, "she has been <u>very</u> grateful indeed…" and I hear a fist smash a face and a bloody-nosed Emile LaGrange rushes past me and out the hotel door to the street.

*Quel drame!*

Later that afternoon, after the hair salon and a sandwich in my room, I am exhausted. The overheard *contretemps* between the two men this morning, and the anxiety over what to expect from Brit this coming evening, has me off balance. I feel between two rather uncomfortable chairs.

But I want to be in Paris. I want to be in my small hotel. And although it is Brit who is most compelling in my reasoning in staying an extra week, it is the *histoire* of Jean-Luc and Isabella being written before me; the fate of Corot's '*Nymphe en Rose*' and its forger, Jillian Spenser; the reconciliation (or not) between Duke, his father, and the enigmatic Elise – all these are so persuasive and all-consuming, that it seems I have no choice. Stay I must.

At 4:45, I am on my way to the taxi stand at the corner. My white suit is crisp, and the discreet bit of gold jewelry I wear is just enough to make me feel adorned and for some reason in charge.

The gallery is already filled, when I arrive. I am greeted once again by Monsieur Fernand who is at the entrance, cordially inviting all the guests into the elegant art-deco building that houses so many beautiful pieces.

'*Diamants en Pluie*' dominates the room, centered on the back wall, the impressive abstract lit from below. It is spectacular. Next to it I see the smaller version. It's there! Right next to its larger twin, only 10'x12'. Beside it, I make out from a distance, the small red 'sold' dot beside it.

He painted it for me, I think, almost stumbling in the emotion this thought brings me. Where is he? Where is Brit?

But I see him, there, on the right side of the room, surrounded, animated, and suddenly, he spies me staring at him. He stops in mid-conversation, excuses himself, and comes to me.

"You always take my breath away," he says in the smallest voice.

"As do you take mine" I reply.

"You see your little picture?"

All I can do is nod and grin and nod some more and grin again.

"It's madness tonight, but tomorrow evening, after the show – that belongs to us."

"Go. Go," I say. "This is your night. Tonight you are the star.

You deserve it all, Brit. Truly. The show is magnificent, particularly, 'Diamonds,'" I whisper. He squeezes both my hands and is off to the group clamoring for his presence.

Elated, relieved by the sweetness he expressed, I wander from painting to painting. His work is impressive. I recognize some of the pieces, the dog and the cabbages on a chair, and the leaves of the trees spilling over the frame. I remember the ocean – the one he described as a feeling of what it is like to be submerged in the blue water. It is there, seeming to undulate underneath one, and infinite in its depths. As I make my way from one visual feeling to another, I am accosted by my ironic and amusing friend, Ray Guild.

A kiss on each cheek, as is *de rigueur* in French social circles.

"You look grand, Madame Elizabeth," he says with a merry twist to his mouth. "So grand!"

"*Merci beaucoup,*" I reply. "You look pretty grand yourself."

"This is quite a show, no?" he says, tucking his arm under mine. "Our boy, Brit, he surely knows how to paint. This..." and he stretches his arm about the room. "This should really put him on the map...not that he doesn't already have a big following...oh, yes indeed. But *Fernand et Fils.* – it's big in this town."

"Where is the *Fils?*" I ask. "Is he here?"

"No way. He doesn't exist. Fernand is a cool old bastard. He knows it sounds like he's been in business as a dynasty... but actually, he's only been here – at this location – for the past five years. The tourists don't know it – the rich Americans and Brazilians...they like the sense of longevity when they buy art. Fernand is no fool."

Around we go and around again. "Madam Elizabeth, do you want to grab a bite?...unless you're waiting for the belle of the ball," Ray says, nodding his head in the direction of Brit.

"What a fine idea," I agree, and both of us with a wave and a blown kiss in Brit's direction, we depart over to the Left Bank and to a restaurant named *L'Esplanade,* near Les Invalides. Napoleon's Tomb is lighted and presents a dramatic backdrop to our really delicious dinner which we have outside under a canopy.

Over a delectable *côte d'agneau* and extraordinarily sweet *petits pois,* and after a round or two of *kirs royals,* Ray has the temerity to ask me how Brit and I 'were doing or doing it,' he says with a laugh, at which I blush.

"You're blush tells me that something is going on, my dear. Now don't dare to deny it. I sensed it from the first."

I don't say anything yet until finally I blurt out, "Well, yes, I do quite like him."

"That's obvious. But it's also obvious that he likes you – although I'm not sure I'd use the word 'like.' Anyway, I'm happy for you both. You're two good people."

"He's mysterious, Ray, Brit is. I find him a bit unknowable."

"Aren't all artists, darling? Unknowable, I mean."

"I guess so. But his past. He reveals so little."

"Well, do you tell all? I would doubt it."

"No. I probably don't. It's just that I worry – he is so attractive, you know...there must have been lots of women..."

"Oh, I don't know. Not all attractive men have 'lots' of women. I only know of one serious relationship he had – oh, a while ago – she's no longer on this earth..."

"I know. He told me she died of cancer."

"Cancer? Then there must have been another one. Poor Brit. Two girlfriends dying on him? Terrible."

"What do you mean, two girlfriends?"

"Oh, you know me. I'm just jesting. Of course there weren't two dying girls. I only know of one. I believe it was a long-term relationship – somewhere in Southern California they lived together – I think her name was Maryanne or Marianna – anyway, her death was mysterious. I heard that she drowned."

"Drowned?" I stop in mid-bite.

"Yes. In the ocean."

"Drowned," I repeat.

"It was all very mysterious."

I can eat no more. I can drink no more. I tell Ray I don't feel too well, and he kindly walks me back several blocks to Hotel Marcel and leaves me on the stoop, deeply devastated.

Brit. Is everything you tell me a fable? Are all your words nothing but lies? Was it cancer? Was it death by drowning? Or was it something else that caused your lover to die? Or were there two deaths in your past life? What is true?

Or not?

# Chapter 24

❧

## A Rainy Day in Paris

Here's that rainy day, all right. I cower under the blanket, staying in bed most of Saturday morning, thinking sad thoughts. Finally, angry at the self-pitying, I rise, dress slowly in the casual slacks and sweater I wore on the plane, and sit on the side of the bed.

There is no way I am going to the grand opening of Brit's art exhibit this evening. I would have no way of really talking to him, and until I clear some of the questions in my head about his past, I would not know what to say to him.

There is always tomorrow…after the next public show…when he said he would give me my painting, and that we would have the evening to ourselves. I cannot bear to see him until then.

Restless, I move to the balcony. The rain is coming down as drizzle. Still, as I open the doors, I see that the windows of building 3, fifth floor, the Frontenac apartment, are covered with damask curtains, but the windows of building 1, fifth floor, at the LaGrange apartment, are open to view, revealing the salon, even through the misty film of rain.

Inside I see the sofa, next to which Sylvie stands, hand upraised. Her husband is before her, half bent toward her. I can hear her shrieking at him over the frantic barking of Schnitzel who is bouncing around at her feet. She is wearing the nasty old bathrobe she seems to live in. The scene is startling in its intensity, enough to make one cringe. It is ugly.

This goes on for some minutes – the yelling – the barking – the raised fists on both sides – until with a loud shout of '*bâtard*,' Sylvie marches from the room, the dog in hot pursuit. Emile LaGrange throws up his hands in defeat and sinks to the couch.

Well, I think. Other people seem to be having a bad day too.

I get out my raincoat from the tiny *armoire* in the corner of my room. I am going to take a walk in the rain. I borrow an umbrella from the stand in the lobby and walk around the corner and down towards Les Invalides, peering in windows. I buy some chocolate covered orange peel in a small sack at the *chocolaterie,* a kind of consolation prize for my mood, and continue walking, trying to tire myself enough to have a nap.

I decide I am really hungry, and reverse my steps heading for *Le Nôtre* where I will select something delectable from their cold case. And oh, yes, a *demi-bouteille* of wine. That too, will help with a nap.

Inside the noted food emporium, as I bend over to inspect the offerings displayed on layers of crushed ice, I sense someone directly next to me doing the same. I turn and, of all people, am face to face with Henriette from the Frontenac *ménage*. She is dressed in a brown raincoat beneath which I see her regular long black dress.

"*Bonjour,* Henriette," I say.

She nods at me with a little smile.

"*Tout va bien?*" I ask.

She gives her head a little shake, then shrugs her ample shoulders.

I turn back to the case and order from the lady behind the

counter a salad of shrimp and chopped hardboiled eggs, and some green beans *vinaigrette*.

I go over to the wine rack to claim a half-bottle when I hear, in French, Henriette and the counter lady speaking. Apparently things are not so good at home, according to Henriette. "Nobody speaks. Madame stays in her room. She won't come out. I have to bring her special food – like this *éclair* – has to be a *éclair café... pas de chocolat, pas de vanille – seullement café...*"

"Like she's pregnant, or something," says the counter lady, at which both start to laugh uncontrollably.

"And Monsieur," continues Henriette. "He is so cold – like he's frozen in time...says nothing...frowns always...Once in awhile, he will tap at her door, and she will call, 'Leave me alone.' Something's going on all right," all this in French which I manage to decipher.

Something's going on all right, and his name is Duke.

On my return to Hotel Marcel, Brigitte at the front desk, gives me my key and two message notes. I wait until I'm in my room before opening either. The first is from Ray. "You looked so sad when I left you last night. I hope it wasn't anything I said. Your friend, RG."

The second note was from Brit. "I hope you come tonight, darling, but if not, tomorrow evening when we'll have time after the gallery closes to be together. I can't wait. Your Brit."

My Brit? I wonder.

I had left the balcony doors open. I go across the room, around the bed, to close them and as I glance out across the street, I notice that the LaGrange windows are still visibly open. Inside the salon are again two figures, only this time I recognize the stocky figure of Kurt as one of the actors in the play I am watching.

It is hard to imagine that this confrontation could be nastier than the one between husband and wife earlier in the day, but indeed, it seems the two men, Emile LaGrange, he of the silver-haired temples, and his thuggish brother-in-law are ready to come to blows. They are physically threatening each other.

I stand there mesmerized as suddenly Kurt hurls himself at the older man, as he had thrown himself at Sasha at the Frontenac's dinner table six months ago. Emile LaGrange hits the floor as Kurt stands over him menacingly. Then the brute kicks him, turns away and leaves the room.

*Mon Dieu!*

The rain begins to pour in sheets and I can see no more. It is just as well because with all the emotion of the day – and last night – I feel quite undone.

Although now it is only late afternoon, I decide to eat my delicacies from *Le Nôtre*. I call downstairs for some utensils and a wine glass, even though I know my small hotel does not permit food in the rooms, (too many crumbs and aging bits and pieces of food) I believe Jean-Luc will honor my request.

And he does.

I sit quietly at the small desk and finish the tasty shrimp and vinegary beans. The wine goes down easily. Then, changing for bed, I finish the last of the *Sauvignon Blanc* against my soft pillows, as I watch the end of an episode of dubbed in French "Law and Order" on TV.

Then comes out the packet of chocolate covered orange peel which I munch on until the very last delicious strip is consumed.

I do not have an ounce of guilt. I deserved the sweet after a rainy day in Paris full of people with unresolved emotion, filled with anger, and totally lacking in love. Oh Brit. Not you. Not you lacking in love. Please, God. Not you.

# Chapter 25

⌒ ⟳ ⌒

## Marianna

It is after 9:00 PM when the show at *Fernand et Fils. Galerie* closes. I have been here only for the last hour, watching Brit engaging with any number of people – critics, a reporter or two, and the buyers. There are several who have purchased his paintings. Many red dots are next to individual pictures, which I am sure pleases Brit and Monsieur Fernand as well.

There is Sasha! He has come to photograph the works of art for a special feature to appear in the French *Vogue*. He is alone. Ray Guild is not here this evening. I see Sasha in front of *'Diamants en Pluie.'* His back is to me as he kneels pointing his camera up. When he gets to his feet, I tap him on the shoulder.

"Well, well. If it isn't Elizabeth." He gives me a big hug. "You look great."

"You too. I hear big things about you, that you are doing a book on the *Façades de Paris*."

"Yes. I'm excited about it. I want to take a lot of shots of that new hotel going up next to Hotel Marcel. It's going to be expensive...4 or 5 stars – I hope Jean-Luc can survive the competition."

"Oh, he will," I say quickly. "It may make business even better for him. His rates are so much cheaper and the location is just as sensational for Hotel Marcel as it is for the pricey new, next-door neighbor. I've noticed all the construction work on the street...have to step over boards and debris... I always try to walk the other direction... and the building...they must have taken over at least five store fronts..."

"I think six..." interjects Sasha.

"And the color," I continue. "It's like alabaster...so white."

"Some sort of processed plastic, I suspect, but it is very dramatic on the street."

"It's really quite amazing."

"How about this picture!" Sasha says, turning to the large abstract, 'Diamants,' before us. "Now that's amazing. Beautiful, no? And I love the small rendition next to it. Somehow that one is more accessible. Both pictures are so...sexy. Funny to say about an abstract."

At this moment, Brit joins us.

He is beaming, looking down at my face, and with a strong pat on Sasha's shoulder, he says, "I am going to take her away. I'm hungry and she better be too." With that, he grabs my hand, swiftly lifts the small 'Diamants' from the wall and pulls me through the remaining people and out the door of the gallery without so much as a goodbye to anyone.

He takes me to *Petrossian,* an elegant caviar and smoked salmon store/restaurant much like *Caviar Kaspia,* except it is on the Left Bank near Hotel Marcel. We are upstairs in the carpeted, rather grand second floor restaurant, where soft French love songs are playing.

Over smoked salmon with capers and toast points and a bottle of champagne, he talks animatedly of the show, of the personalities of the different buyers, of the celebrities who came – a French actor

and his wife a well-known *chanteuse* – "they bought *'La Mer.'*"
Brit is overflowing with positive feelings. He is elated – as well he
should be – at the success of his exhibition.

"All your hard work...it certainly has paid off!" I say as
enthusiastically as I can. I know I have been distant with him. I
know what is to come...my inquisition...and I know it may change
things between us forever.

We take his car – with my painting on the back seat. He opens
the windows, although it is a short drive to the hotel. The rain from
yesterday has cleared the air of humidity. The soft breeze is sweet,
and a full moon pours light from a fresh sky.

In my bedroom, Brit takes my little *'Diamants'* and places the
picture against the pillows on my pristine bed. I have turned on
the bedside lamp, and it illuminates the picture's brushstrokes and
details in an extraordinary way. The picture is breathtaking.

Brit takes me by the shoulders and says, "You have been pretty
remote this evening."

I nod. Then I blurt out, "Died of cancer? That's what you
told me...how it came on very fast...that she hadn't felt well. All
very sad."

Brit looks staggered. "What?"

We are standing face to face. The bed lamp illuminates
our features, his, suddenly haggard and chagrinned, before my
accusatory onslaught.

"Ray Guild told me her death was actually a mystery."

"He did, did he?" After a long pause, Brit says, "He was right."

"Why did you make up such a story...cancer the cause of her
death?"

"Because I felt there was no way really to dispute it, for one
thing. Cancer – it has such a terminal ring to it. There would be
no questions."

"You mean no one would believe you could have possibly lied,"

I say coldly. "Everyone would 'buy' your fairy tale?" I say, sinking down on the bed dispirited.

Brit looks at me reproachfully, then slowly, he says, "Yes, I lied."

"Oh, Brit." I am close to tears. "Deception is so ugly."

"I know," he says solemnly. Then slowly he begins. "We lived kind of removed from general society...I thought it...cancer... was the simplest thing to say. And I knew Marianna...she was such a proud person...I knew she wouldn't want anyone to know she had taken her own life. It seemed best at the time to make her death something as common...as a cancer."

"Taken her own life?" I am deeply moved. And appalled.

Brit, who has been standing, looking down at me on my bed, sits down on the coverlet, not close to me, but near.

"Marianna committed suicide," he says with a sigh. Then, "She had a very bloody miscarriage. I can never go through again, watching a person I love in such pain and despair." He shakes his head at the memory. "It tipped her over the edge – she wasn't young, and in her earlier life she had had an abortion, about which she always felt guilty. The miscarriage was the final straw. It did something to her."

Brit stands up and starts to pace. "We were living by the sea in Southern California – a little shed house by the beach – each working away. One night - there was only a sliver of a moon – I went to sleep – when I woke, she was gone. I went out calling. I knew something was terribly wrong." There is a long pause. "And there was her body by the edge of the waves. She had walked out into the surf until she drowned and was washed up on the sand at dawn."

Then he sinks onto the bed again. His head is in his hands. "Afterwards, I had a vasectomy."

Later, putting *'Diamants'* aside, we lie on my bed, our limbs gilded under the golden light of the full moon, and by the sparks that come this night from the Eiffel Tower. He cries in my arms, before we make love – then slowly, powerfully, we are overcome with desire.

And I believe him, his story of Marianna so poignant, his tone so full of grief, his vulnerability so exposed. I find it impossible for a man such as Brit to concoct such a story of miscarriage, abortion, and suicide. These words would not come easily to him.

He has allowed me into a private place of his own, a place I have longed to be. His tears have touched my own cheek – and my heart.

And oh, yes. I believe him.

Absolutely.

# Chapter 26

❦

## Quiche Lorraine

Brit left me near 6:00 AM. I am warm in our bed, filled with the scents and sense of love, languid, happy. Before he left this morning, he promised to take me to Barbizon, the small village outside of Paris where the Impressionist painters plied their trade under the dulcet light of northern France, in the early 1800s.

We plan to go mid-week and spend the night at Hôtellerie du Bas-Brèau, a superb country inn, frequented in the past by the likes of Margaret Thatcher, Kissinger, de Gaulle. Not that all these political figures matter, but the place obviously attracts discriminating people. It must be special.

And it will be special because Brit will be there. With me.

The phone rings. Brit?

"*Bonjour, jolie madame.*" It is Jean-Luc.

"Why, hello there."

"I call for a reason. It's important," he says.

"I can come downstairs."

"*Non.* I am at home. Brigitte is covering the front desk. I take today to ask you over to *déjeuner* with Isabella and myself. You know I love to cook – but it's important because I know you are concerned about us – Isabella and me – *non?*"

"Well...yes, I have been a little worried..." I say, sitting up against the pillows. "You two haven't seemed...as close..."

"I know, I know," he says rapidly. "But there is a reason. That's why I want you to come today. We both want you. Please. A little after noon, yes?"

"Yes," I say with a little laugh. "*Bien sûr.* I'll be there...over the *pharmacie.*" I had been to his chic little apartment before on my last visit.

"*Bien,*" he says and hangs up.

I am glad to be going. I want an answer to my anxiety about the state of their affairs. Still lolling in bed, I look across to my beautiful, small '*Diamants.*' It seems to smile back at me, as I lie here on my personal cloud nine.

I decide on the white pants suit and on the way to lunch, I pick up a bag of macaroons from *Le Nôtre* for a luncheon dessert. At the top of the stairs next to the *pharmacie,* I ring the doorbell which Isabella answers.

"Elizabeth, Elizabeth," she says embracing me. I hand her the confections, which she receives with burbles of delight. The living room/kitchen with the dark blue couch, white walls, and posters of American jazz greats smells of something wonderful cooking in the oven, next to which Jean-Luc is standing proudly.

"Come. Sit down." The small table by the window is set for three, and he brings over a bottle of cold *Sauvignon Blanc* which he pours into the wine glasses at each place setting. "A toast," he says, and we raise glasses and clink.

"I want to get straight to the point," Jean-Luc says, as he sits down beside us. "I know you saw Isabella in the Mini-Cooper with...LaGrange." His lips curl in anger. "I also know you are aware of the fight I had with that man and that I bloodied his nose."

I am nodding at all this.

"Well, he deserved it because he has been blackmailing Isabella…"

"Blackmailing?" I am astonished. "How?"

"By threatening to reveal her past to me and to the world."

I turn to Isabella who is listening intently to her lover's explanation.

"It's because I am not exactly who I say I am…" she says, her voice timid. "I am from Sitges – yes. That's true – the small beach town near Barcelona –but I was raised by my uncle as my father…" She then turns to Jean-Luc. "Help me explain, please, *chéri…*"

"Isabella's true father was a Basque man – her mother Spanish… she had Isabella when she was very young. Isabella's real father was a gypsy…they range all over the Pyrenees and many are thieves. He was one." Jean-Luc touches Isabella's hand.

"When I was two years old," she says, "my mother decided I should be…how you say…"

"Raised," says Jean-Luc.

"Yes, yes," she continues, "raised by her brother who had an antique shop in the small village on the coast…the Costa Brava… He and his wife had no children and were happy to take me …"

"And they loved her. How could they not?" Jean-Luc says, eyeing Isabella with such affection.

"And I loved them. They were my real family." Her eyes filled with tears. "I never saw my real father again. He was killed in some robbery…and my mother died soon after…"

"Oh, my dear," I say. "How hard for you."

"At first. But not really. They were so good to me. I loved them. And when Monsieur LaGrange came into the shop and bought so much from my father – really my uncle, but I always felt he was my father – and Monsieur LaGrange was kind, my father asked him to watch over me. He told him my whole story which now that man...Monsieur LaGrange..."she says with bitterness and sarcasm, "he holds this over my head like a sword, demanding I give up Jean-Luc, insisting I lie with him in bed, threatening to tell everybody, even my boss..."

At this point Jean-Luc is on his feet, fists clenched. "*Quel homme vicieux!*" He says furiously. "*Assez!*" And he marches over to the stove to check his creation. "*Il faut manger.*" He says reaching into the stove and retrieving the *Quiche Lorraine*. But his mood is palpably angry. One can feel it across the room.

He pulls a *salade composé* from the ice-box – lettuces, strips of red pepper, artichoke hearts – pours over a *vinaigrette* and brings this to our table. He returns to the kitchen, cuts up the fragrant ham and cheese pie and brings this to us on three large plates.

We begin to eat in silence, helping ourselves to the salad, consuming the exquisitely rich and delicious pie. More wine is sipped. Macaroons are produced, and coffee poured, but even through this gracious repast, I sense the boiling anger in Monsieur Marcel.

I finally turn to him and say, "Jean-Luc, I know how upset you are...how truly furious you are with that awful man who threatens your dearest Isabella...but I hope you can keep that anger in check..."

"I don't know if I can."

"You must. It does no good. Hate him if you have to. But for heaven's sake, please, please don't do anything about it."

As I leave, to break the bitter mood, I say to him, "You're going to need a class in 'anger management'...like La Grange's brother-in-law, Kurt Vronsky...if you're not careful," at which we all laugh, hug, and laugh again.

As I go down the stairs to the street, I am not laughing at all. Cool it, Jean-Luc, I think. You had really better cool it.

# Chapter 27

❦

## A Rude Awakening

I wake late in the night to the sound of a woman screeching. It comes from the street below, rising up with bloodcurdling force. Hastily, I step from my bed out onto the balcony and see below me, in the light of a street lamp, the figure of a woman with red-hair in a shabby bathrobe, mouth open and screaming. She pounds her chest and shifts from foot to foot in obvious agony.

Sylvie Vronsky LaGrange!

God in heaven, what's happened?

And then I hear the sound of that elegant wail of the French police car braying like a donkey, 'Hee Haw, Hee Haw,' cutting through the dark night, rising in volume as it nears and pulls to a stop next to Sylvie. And who steps out of the car? René Poignal himself, trench coat belted.

So late at night? Does he never stop his duties? Does he ever sleep?

I watch as he approaches Sylvie carefully. The two other uniformed policemen with him enter the large portal of apartment building 1 and presumably go up to the LaGrange duplex on the fourth and fifth floors.

René has his arm around Sylvie, who is now moaning. I can see the glisten of her tears in the lamplight.

Suddenly, I am aware that Duke Davis has joined me on his balcony.

"Good lord," he says, rubbing his eyes. "What's happening?"

"Something pretty terrible, I guess."

We stand there side by side in the dark. René Poignal is guiding Sylvie, whose steps stumble, back into the building. For minutes, the street is quiet.

"Have you seen him again?" I ask. "Your father?"

"Yes!" Duke's tone of voice is strong. "He has come to *Le Club* twice now. We are able to talk between sets."

"Really. What do you talk about?"

"Mostly about mother...He is curious what happened to her. I think he really did care for her."

"I know he did, Duke. I'm sure for him it was a grand passion."

"I hope so," he says wistfully. "He says he wants to bring his wife one night. She's having a hard time – even with the idea of me."

I'll just bet she is, I think. Elise is a pretty prim character. But I say, "That would be something."

We are quiet together. Dawn is coming up around the edges of the sky. Finally, he says, "Do you think it would be...easier...if you were there too? You know...another woman?"

"Me?" I am taken aback.

"Yes, of course, you."

"Well...I guess so...maybe..." I am not at all sure. "You'd better ask...your father."

Our attention is drawn back to the street as another police car arrives wailing its wail, followed by a service truck with an attachment at the back. The attachment is flat with what looks to be a folded metal ladder lying upon it. Three men are scurrying about positioning the apparatus. Slowly but surely, we see the ladder-like structure unfold automatically and rise slowly to the fifth floor balcony of apartment building 1.

On that balcony two policemen appear, leaning over, looking down at the unfolding ladder, as if it were some strange snake ascending from the street. One of them is smoking, which makes me run to get a cigarette and lighter.

The ladder is now in position. A flat, metal surface appears at its top, extending like an arm. The two policemen disappear inside and return carrying a stretcher covered in a tarpaulin, which they load onto the flat surface of the arm.

Good Lord. A body! Kurt? Emile LaGrange? Someone else?

The whole contraption reverses itself and the stretcher is conveyed down to the pavement, the ladder refolding itself. A new van has arrived below marked *Morgue*. I see a man in a white jacket enter the building, a doctor for Sylvie? To attend to her hysterics?

The van, now loaded with the stretcher, pulls away from the curb. As it does so, I see Kurt emerge from the apartment entrance with Schnitzel on his leather leash. He walks toward the Champ de Mars, cool as a cucumber, striding along carefree, as though nothing in the LaGrange apartment has happened. Nothing at all.

Kurt is not the body. Kurt is alive. LaGrange?

Now that is another story, one I pray does not include Jean-Luc Marcel.

# Chapter 28

꧁ ꧂

## Broken Glass

It is 6:00 AM Tuesday morning, the 19th of May. I have continued to watch the scene below. Large shards of broken glass have descended from the balcony on the fifth floor of apartment building 1, by way of the ladder–like structure. Some of the edges of the glass pieces are tinged red.

Next to the car with the ladder attachment, on the street below, I see a glazier van pull up and stop. Two men from the cab of the van extract a large pane of glass and place it on the arm to ascend to the fifth floor. It looks to be a large, full length mirror. It slowly ascends the side of the building as the two *vitriers* enter the building to go upstairs, presumably to install it.

What goings on! I think, as I see René Poignal come out of the apartment building 1 and cross the street to Hotel Marcel. I rush to dress to go down to breakfast, but for a vastly more important reason than food, no, to see what's happening!

Brigitte is at the desk in the lobby. I can hear male voices from Jean-Luc's office, as I ask her for coffee at the salon table.

I sit there, tapping my fingers, awaiting what? when the two men, René and Jean-Luc appear. They are extremely solemn, and when René leaves to go back to his duties Jean-Luc comes to sit with me.

"What's happened?" I ask. "I've been watching the commotion on the street – from Sylvie's screeches to a body coming down the side of the building to a new glass mirror going up. What in blazes happened?"

"Emile LaGrange is dead."

"Oh, God." It's all I can say.

"I am under suspicion."

"You?"

"Everyone knows the hatred we had for each other. Of course, I would be a suspect." This Jean-Luc says so emphatically that I do a double take.

"It's not true," I exclaim.

"Of course it's not true," he says, looking at me hard. "But as René announced, I have motive – and that counts for something."

I take a long pull at my coffee. "How did he die? Was it the glass?"

"*Non*. He was strangled. It was in the master bedroom on the fifth floor. His neck was almost cut in half and he fell back into the long mirror."

"Where was Sylvie?"

"She was in a guest room. They had been fighting – a big fight – according to her. She admitted she had slapped him, but she could not have strangled him – doesn't have the strength."

"And the fight? What was it about?"

Jean-Luc gives me a quizzical glance. "You know, Elizabeth. Not what was it about, but who?"

"Isabella." He merely nods.

I take another long sip of coffee. "What about Kurt?"

"He claims he was in his attic room. You know, in those buildings there are two elevators, one to the apartment and a separate one at the back that goes to the attic. It was built that way so servants could come and go without bothering the residents. Pretty outdated, but that's the way those older art-deco apartments were built."

We sit silent for a minute, then I say, "You know, Kurt has motive too. I saw him push Emile LaGrange to the ground in the salon yesterday. When he was down, Kurt even kicked him."

"He did?" Jean-Luc's face lights up. "You saw this? That is something René has to know. You're sure?"

"Absolutely. You know me and the balcony and my binoculars," I say ruefully. "It was yesterday afternoon. Kurt is brutal. He surely would have the strength to strangle."

"But strangle with what. It was obvious to the police that there was a rope or chain of some sort that cut the man's throat."

"A knife?"

"No, apparently the edge of the wound was uneven – like it was sawed."

"Ugh!" I say.

"Enough of the gory details," Jean-Luc says, smiling for the first time this morning. "I'm going to find René."

And he leaves me sitting there just as a basket of croissants arrive, warm and inviting.

I have lost my appetite. Even the delicate, buttery aroma cannot whet it and entice me to take a bite, for all I can picture is Emile LaGrange, lying in a pool of blood, surrounded with broken glass.

# Chapter 29

❦

## Music in the Night

On my way back to the *ascenseur,* I see Jillian Spenser, with Amelia in tow, run into the hotel. Brigitte is at the desk.

"What was going on last night?" she asks breathlessly of the young Scandinavian.

"I am not sure, Madame," the girl responds.

"But the police...the sirens..."

"I know," says Brigitte. "I was not here at the time, but I understand there was a crime."

I come forward from the rear.

"Yes, Jillian, an awful crime. A man was killed."

"Crikey!" Jillian says, then, blushing, she says, "Do you know who?"

"A man in the building next to yours."

"Oh, no! That gives me the shivers." She clutches Amelia to her side. "Have they caught who did it?"

"Not yet," I say. "Come. Sit. Would you like a coffee?"

"No thank you. But I will sit down for a moment. I feel quite undone by this news. Right next door!" and she pulls her daughter beside her onto the couch in the little lounge adjoining the salon.

"How are things going?" I venture. "Have you found a gallery for your pictures?"

"Not yet…nothing definite, but there is one on the Left Bank over in St. Germain that has shown interest. They quite like what I do," she says with a deprecating smile.

"That's great," I say. "You know, I have an artist friend who shows his work in a gallery on the Right Bank – rue St. Honoré," I say pointedly. "Perhaps I could bring him to view your watercolors. Would you want that? He might be able to help."

Of course I really want Brit to take a hard look at the Corot.

"Why that would be wonderful," Jillian says, her face alight with hope.

"Would it be convenient to come…maybe tomorrow?"

"Lovely. Teatime, as usual," she says, as Amelia chimes in, "And maybe could you bring Duke?"

With that I smile and say I'll try.

Upstairs, as I shake off the unpleasant facts of the early morning, and at the same time embrace the idea of having Brit appraise the Corot, I have not one, but three phone calls.

The first is from Sue. We make a lunch date for tomorrow at *Caviar Kaspia*. "I have a mountain of news to tell you," I say to her, at which she replies, "Tell me, tell me," and I say, "No, tomorrow we'll have the time and place to *bavard*. We do love to gossip." She laughs, as she hangs up.

The second call is Brit. He asks me if Friday would be a good day for us to go to Barbizon. "I want to take you to the seat of the Impressionists and to that beautiful inn, Hôtellerie du Bas-Brèau. We can spend the night. What do you think?"

"I think it sounds grand! I'd love to." After this morning the idea of having a day away from this particular Paris avenue is a fine thing. "And I have a question for you…as an artist. Would you be willing – or have the time – to have tea with me across the street at

Jillian Spenser's to evaluate her Corot?" I have told Brit the whole story of the British lady and possible forger.

Brit burst out laughing. "To catch a thief?" he says.

"Maybe. Around 5:00 tomorrow afternoon?"

"Sounds good to me...even just to see you. Bye, my love," and he rings off.

The minute I hang up the phone, it rings again.

"Forget something?" I say.

"Er...*Non.*" There is a pause. "Elizabeth?"

"*Oui,*" I say automatically. I recognize right away that it is Pierre Frontenac.

"I know it is very late to ask, but could you possibly come with me to *Le Club* again? *Ce soir?* I have persuaded *ma femme* to come with me to hear Duke play violin and bass. She has been...*très inconfortable*...*non*...even angry about the whole idea of Duke... you can understand...but finally she has agreed to 'face the music.' Heh, heh," he laughs at his little joke.

"I guess I can join you. Yes, if you think I can help."

"*Je crois...*I think you can because, as Duke says, another woman...you can be *sympathique.*"

And a man can't? I think.

"Okay," I say.

"Excellent," he says, voice rising. "I will collect you a little before 9:00...I mean we will collect you...she and I."

This should be one evening to remember.

And it turns out to be.

Pierre arrives in the lobby with a pale-faced Elise just before 9:00. Her hand in mine feels papery, as she offers it in a handshake. Her lips are compressed and her long nose looks as if she smelled something rotten.

We make our way to a taxi stand. Elise says nothing in the drive to the *boîte,* while Pierre tries to converse about the weather, about the noise and drama in the LaGrange apartment, but he is circumspect and unemotional in tone, saying almost anything to break the silence.

"I did not care for Monsieur LaGrange," he says formally. "But I did not wish him dead."

"Somebody did," I say sardonically.

"Monsieur Marcel?"

"Oh, no. No. Jean-Luc disliked him – in fact he couldn't stand him – but I know Jean-Luc. He could not possibly have been so brutal."

"That *beau-frère*...what's his name...?"

"Kurt."

"Yes. Kurt. He could be. He is *bestial*."

Bestial. The perfect word in French <u>or</u> English.

We arrive at the top of the stairs to the entrance to *Le Club*. At this point Elise says, looking at the dark stairwell, "I'm not going down there."

"Please, Elise," Pierre says. "You promised."

"I said *peut-être. Seulement peut-être.*" And then in more French, "I want no part of this...this betrayal."

"Elise," I say. "It was 20 years ago, a totally different time for both of you. Pierre has been a loyal husband ever since."

"I don't know about that," she remarks. Pierre takes her hand. He gently leads her to the top of the stairs. "This has to happen sooner or later," he says softly, and slowly, oh, so slowly, we start to descend into the dark.

I am following behind the two of them. She glances back but sees no escape because of my presence.

The first set is in full swing, the noise loud, complex, with a strong saxophone. Duke's bass keeps tempo and the piano is all over the place.

The song is American music of the south, "Sweet Georgia

Brown." After several stanzas Duke puts aside his bass, the drummer starts with the snare drum, the sax subsides, and Duke's violin takes over the melody in an astonishing, virtuoso riff that brings down the house.

Elise has her hand to her mouth, eyes wide. She is very still. There is an expression of wonder in her whole persona, sitting straight, motionless. I look at Pierre. He is smiling at her. I realize, for both of them, music holds a special appeal. It is present at every *diner* that I have observed. It could be the reconciling factor.

The set finishes, Duke strides over to our table. There is nothing tentative in his demeanor as he approaches. As he nears, I turn to Elise, saying, "Here comes the future. There's no room now for the past," and I quietly leave them to their encounter with a son/ stepson that neither could have possibly expected.

Moving between the tables, up the steps, and out I go into a Paris night full of promise. *Bonne chance*, I think. *Bonne chance.*

# Chapter 29

❧

## Jean-Baptiste-Camille Corot

I have a delightful lunch with Sue at *Caviar Kaspia,* (where else!) at mid-day Wednesday. We gossip our heads off, mostly about our own racy pasts, old loves, new ones (Brit), Sue refers to him as 'your artist,' and the problems of her son's divorce. I tell her the saga of the street where I live. And it is quite a story to report.

The murder of Emile LaGrange, the suspicion on Jean-Luc's head, the shrieking Sylvie, the broken glass, all comes pouring out of me with much embellishment. I even describe seeing Kurt nonchalantly walking the dog after the event.

Then it's on to the evening at *Le Club,* the fact that Elise was there, that Duke was in fine form, that I left them to themselves…

"You left them? You missed the best part," says Sue, laughing. "I wouldn't have been able to leave. I'd have been too curious."

"Oh, I had to go. They needed some privacy. It's so sensitive. How would you feel if you were Elise with suddenly a stepson and he happens to be black," I say vehemently.

"Of course. Of course. I'm only kidding. Do you have any idea how the meeting went?"

"None. No idea at all."

We finish our lunch of an exquisitely fresh king crab salad both of us ordered, and our carafe of vodka, and over coffee and a raspberry tart I say how sad I am at the thought of leaving Paris again.

"You still have 10 days."

"It's never enough...and Brit. How do I leave Brit?"

"You'll just have to come back," says Sue reassuringly. "You always do, you know," and she leans over and kisses me on the cheek.

A little before 5:00 PM Brit picks me up at the hotel. He is wearing a gray sweater, the color of his eyes and hair, and it almost hurts to look at him. I find him that irresistible.

We cross the street, hand in hand. I have asked Duke to join us, and he promises he will be there, but not until a bit later. Jillian greets us effusively – for her. Brit represents 'possibilities' for her future, and she is particularly welcoming to him. Besides he is a handsome man.

The tea table is laid out before us. Amelia, after saying a sweet hello, sits reading quietly in the corner, happy at the thought of Duke's arrival.

As the kettle starts to whistle on the stove, before Jillian pours our tea into the porcelain cups, she shuts it off and takes Brit to the stand holding her pictures.

I see him inspecting them thoughtfully. "Really quite lovely," he says. "I like the water...the way you treat it." Turning to her, he says, "I paint a lot of waterscapes...don't know what else to call them. Water is so elemental, so necessary and has so many faces... or facets, I guess."

"Oh, I so agree," Jillian gushes, delighted that this gentleman seems to understand her artistry.

At this moment, there is a knock at the door and Duke is there, bag of macaroons from *Le Nôtre* in hand. Amelia is on her feet, running to greet him, and he presents her with the cookie bag. She is obviously joyful to see him and share the macaroons.

Before we sit down at the table, as Jillian reheats the kettle, Brit spots the small Corot in its ornate golden frame. "Is that a Corot?" he asks Jillian.

"It is."

"It's beautiful."

"'*Nymphe en Rose*,'" Jillian says. "Her name was Jeanette Moreau, the daughter of a friend of Corot's. Later, she married a British man and their daughter married into the Spenser family. It was eventually left to me."

Brit has picked it up and is inspecting it carefully. "Corot's brushstrokes are so distinct, and yet, the whole has an ethereal quality. Interesting." Brit even spends several seconds looking intently at the back of the canvas.

"I'm very fond of the picture," Jillian says. "That lovely girl is almost part of the family, right, Amelia?" at which the child nods affirmatively. Then, as she pours the tea, Jillian remarks, almost offhand, "I may have to sell it."

"No," I say. "Why on earth…"

"It's a matter of money," she interjects. "You know, good old money. Paris is expensive, God knows…and my pittance from Amelia's father…well, it's not much."

I am completely surprised at the frankness of this repressed woman, one so proper. I always thought that 'money' was not considered to be anybody's business but one's own, and to discuss it, impolite. At least in certain circles.

"You should have no trouble. It should bring a good price," Brit says as we move to sit at the table. Amelia has already spread out her macaroons on a plate, which sits amid the other teacakes.

"I'm not sure how to go about it…selling it. Do I take it to a gallery? Do you think…where you exhibit…?"

Brit quickly interrupts. "I don't think Fernand would be interested. He is into more modern expression," and he glances at me. I know that Fernand would love to get his hands on a Corot, but only a real one, not a fake.

"Have you thought of auction?" Brit suggests.

"I really haven't thought that much about it yet at all."

"Well," Brit says, munching on a lime-green macaroon, "Have you heard of the Drouot Auction House? It's famous…not far from the Boulevard Haussmann."

"Why yes. I believe I have."

"They auction off all sorts of things – antiques, old books, treasures of all sorts and including a large fine arts department. They hold auctions twice a week in all categories. I think they would be excited to have a Corot to offer."

"How does it work? I mean…do I just bring it over there and go to the fine arts office? And how do they appraise it? I have no idea of its worth. I've never had it evaluated," says Jillian.

My foot, I think. Of course she knows its value.

"Drouot will do that. You will agree to a base price, and if the auction does not come up to that number…you know…if nobody bids that high, you have the right to take the painting back or accept the lower price. Either way, you will have to pay the 10 percent commission to Drouot."

"That doesn't seem fair," Jillian bristles. "The 10 percent."

"Oh, it's eminently fair," Brit responds. "After all, they have given your picture publicity and a venue in which to show it at its best. They have supplied a number of possible buyers. They have appraised it for you…I think they well deserve the fee."

"Of course," Jillian says, backpedalling. "I wasn't thinking."

Through all this conversation, I watch Amelia and Duke. They are teasing each other over their macaroons, obviously drawn to each other as young friends. Duke has an open charm. I only hope he can build this kind of rapport with Elise Frontenac. Perhaps over time.

"I think I'll go over there – to Drouot," Jillian is saying. "Where did you say it was?"

"It's in the 9th arrondissement. You can't miss it – on rue Drouot. It has, I think, 15 or 16 salesrooms where you can wander about and decide your bid on something you want. Of course, the auction room itself is a large auditorium."

"I'm going over there tomorrow," Jillian says decisively. "Just to look. If I like what I see, then I'll bring over the painting. I hate to let her go." She eyes the picture across the room. "My '*Nymphe en Rose*'...but reality...it rears its ugly head."

Teatime is done and we rise to leave with pleasant goodbyes and thanks for this time spent together.

"Thank you," she says to Brit, "for seeing my pictures and for suggesting the auction house."

"Good luck with that," Brit says, while shaking her hand as he glances at the Corot.

She seems to hold his hand a little too long, I think. Hey. Let it go.

And we are out of there. Duke has given Amelia a little hug on leaving. His face is happy. As we cross the street, I ask him how things are going.

"Fine," is his reply.

"And with Elise?"

He grins at me. "Better...slowly...but better." With a little wave, he is lost in traffic.

As we reach Brit's car, which is parked near the hotel, he turns and takes me by both shoulders. Looking me straight in the eye, he says, "That Corot is a forgery...and a good one. I'll explain how I am sure its fake at another time because I have to get all these..." he gestures toward his car which is loaded with pictures large and small, "I have to get these over to the *Fernand* gallery. So many of the pictures have been sold that the place is virtually empty of my work. Monsieur Fernand needs a new supply." With this he beams with pride.

"That's so fabulous, Brit."

"And so now, my love, I'm off. But I think you should tell that police detective and maybe Jean-Luc about the forged painting and that it may be at Drouot. I'm sure they'd be most interested."

He gives me a long kiss, right there on the street. But it's Paris and nobody notices. "I'll pick you up early Friday morning and we'll blow this town together. Can't wait!" And he climbs in his car and is gone.

Me too, Brit. I can't wait either, but in the meantime I have to find Jean-Luc and René Poignal. All of a sudden a strange thought occurs…no, more like a question.

Is Spenser Jillian's married name? Is Amelia's father a Spenser? If so wouldn't it have been <u>he</u> to inherit the Corot? Or does she use her maiden name for her work?

Ah. Another mystery to solve and how I relish it.

# Chapter 30

## Truth Be Told

As I enter the hotel, I notice that the new hotel next door is being worked on, even this late in the evening. Workmen are beginning to dismantle some of the framework that supported them on different levels as they had installed windows and outer cornices. The building begins to show its white alabaster skin in all its glory.

There are three trucks at the curb collecting boards and wires and all manner of detritus. Lord what a mess! The Grand Opening is scheduled to take place on Sunday evening, so probably the men will be working well into this night.

I see Jean-Luc in his office, the door to which is wide open. Ah, I think. I must arrange a meeting with René Poignal and with Jean-Luc, of course, and I sidle into the room. Although he is on the phone, he beckons me to come in. I do, shutting the door behind me, and sit on the empty chair.

He is speaking rapidly in French about the building next door, from what I can glean. I gather that Hotel Marcel was one of the first edifices approached by the hotel conglomerate in the beginning, but he had been adamant in his refusal to sell his property, apparently much to the dismay of the owners of The

Majestic. That is the name of the new grand establishment, ready and waiting to open so soon.

Hanging up, Jean-Luc lets out a huge sigh and says, "They never give up, those fellows. Still trying to buy me out...they say I'll soon be out of business...but I told them I can stand the competition and to leave me alone."

Then, eyeing me, he says, "You look as if you are about to burst," which of course I am.

"I have so much news, Monsieur. About Jillian... and I really think Detective René would be most intrigued."

"*Vraiment?* Excellent. He always said you were something of a little inspector yourself." And Jean-Luc's hand is already on his phone.

A meeting is arranged for the next morning at breakfast time. Both men have plans for this night, so I hasten over to *La Terrasse* for their *omelet au gruyère* and a glass of wine. Later, in my room, I make notes of exactly what transpired at Jillian's and of Brit's assessment of the Corot, although he has yet to give me details.

Before bed, I step out on the balcony for a final look at the Eiffel Tower and see Kurt on the street with dog leash in hand. What I never noticed before is that the tether to Schnitzel, which is made of a dark leather, seems to have metal studs on it. I can see them sparkle in the light as he walks by the street lamp. Only for a second they gleam.

Why it's a leash strong enough to handle a mastiff, a bit of overkill for walking a lap dog in a Paris park, wouldn't you think? Curious.

On Thursday, I am down in the salon early. As I drink the *café au lait*, René Poignal, ubiquitous trench coat still belted, comes in the lobby. I have yet to see Jean-Luc, but René approaches my seat with an enthusiastic "Bonjour, Madame," sits himself down and says," I understand you have news for me."

"Indeed I do. Shall we wait for Jean-Luc?" But there is no need, for the gentleman in question appears at the lobby door.

The three of us retire to the office in the back. Jean-Luc sits at his desk. I take the only chair. René closes the office door and leans back against it.

"Before you say anything, Madame...and to you as well, Monsieur...you both have to realize that Jean-Luc and Isabella – she is complicit too - are still suspects in the murder of LaGrange."

"No, *non, ce n'est pas vrai,*" both Jean-Luc and I say in unison.

René raises his hand to hush us. "I'm afraid it's true. Jean-Luc you admit you had motive..."

"But what weapon? I have no weapon, and there is no way I'm able to strangle that man with my bare hands."

"The problem is...you could have picked up a weapon - something on the street – with all that building material next door...a rope, a strip of heavy plastic...there is no way he was strangled by hands choking him. It was much more brutal than that – almost like a jagged saw..."

I wince. "But how would Jean-Luc possibly get into the apartment in the middle of the night?"

"And I have an alibi. Isabella and I were home in bed!" Jean-Luc says triumphantly.

René dismisses this with a wave of his hand. "Really, Jean-Luc...you two cover for each other? I think not. But you're right about getting into the building. I guess you could have rung the doorbell..." But even René has to smile at this. "I don't like to think these things, but I have to be thorough...careful...cover all bases, as they say in America..."

"Do you have suspicions about Kurt?" I ask quite suddenly.

"We know he is violent. We know he and LaGrange did not get along...but murder? It seems unlikely."

"Why?" I say.

"There is no known actual fight between the two that we know of."

"I know Emile was furious with Kurt because Kurt told me that he was seeing Isabella behind my back. Emile hated being ratted out by Kurt and having to get in a fight with me," says Jean-Luc.

"Well, I do know of a very real confrontation between LaGrange and Kurt," I interrupt. "I saw from my balcony a great fight between them only a couple of days ago. They were yelling at each other and raising fists, and Kurt pushed Emile to the ground and then he kicked him! While the man was down!"

"You saw this?"

"Absolutely. With my binoculars."

"Would you be willing to testify to this?"

"Yes," I say, gulping. "And you know Kurt has a key. He goes up to his attic room by the back elevator, not the one in front of the building that goes up to the LaGrange apartment. It's separate. And he must have a key because he has to take the dog out for his walk several times a day."

René, who has been leaning against the door all through this, suddenly begins to pace in the very small space.

"And there's something else. I just thought of it," I say, getting up from my chair with excitement. "It's possible. It's possible."

"What's possible," the two men say together.

"The leash!"

"The leash?"

"René, it's heavy. It's made of leather. It's strong enough to manage an attack dog – so ludicrous for a little Shih Tzu, but most important, it has metal studs scattered the length of it – I guess for decoration -"

"*Mon Dieu. C'est possible.* Madame this is important information. I will take the leash into custody right away...and check for DNA. With studs, there might be blood residue..."

Ugh, I think.

"I'll get going immediately," he says, tightening his belt.

"Wait, please, René. There is another matter. About Jillian Spenser. I had an artist friend of mine – a very good artist - come to tea with me at her apartment. He saw a small Corot portrait there in an elaborate gold frame. I had him inspect it without her knowing and he determined that it's a very good forgery. He also suggested she auction it at the Drouot Auction House. And she plans to do so, probably next week. She needs the money. You should warn them when they appraise it that it might be fake.

"And when she goes there for the auction, we can pick her up!" René is elated.

"I'll have more about the forgery in a couple of days and will let you know what to look for."

"Madame, you are doing my work for me," René says, coming forward and embracing me. "You should be in law enforcement," and with a salute to Jean-Luc and a big smile, he leaves the office.

Jean-Luc is on his feet. "I can't believe this. What a relief. It has to be Kurt. He is *tellement vicieux* -a real criminal at heart. Elizabeth, we must celebrate!"

"Do you think it's too soon for that," I say with a smile.

"*Non, non.* Never soon enough for caviar and champagne. Isabella and I will take you to Petrossian," which makes me grin from ear to ear as he waltzes me around the crowded room with necessarily tiny steps.

# Chapter 31

❧

## Barbizon

It is a glorious Friday morning. Brit calls before 9:00, as I pack a small case for our trip out of town. I am wearing jeans, my light blue sweater, and a big grin.

He arrives and we barrel out of Paris in his trusty Peugeot, on a northern route toward what Brit calls 'the painter's village', Barbizon. "It's close to the forest of Fontainebleau. A lot of small villages ring the woods, and in the mid-1800s the place was a magnet for any landscape painter worth his salt...Rousseau, Millet, and of all people, our friend Corot!"

"Speaking of whom, just what did you see in Jillian's '*Nymphe en Rose*' that made you believe it a forgery?"

"Well, two things really. One, the signature. Corot was very precise. Jillian's rendition of his moniker was...well wavy and the final 't' had a very uncharacteristic tilt. And number two – the canvas. It is not new, but it's one that has been stripped down, some old painting scraped off of it, which is typical of how many fake copies are produced. Jillian painted on a relatively clean piece of canvas, but one that hardly comes from the 1800s. And it had a smell. A chemical smell. No, there's no question it is fake...pretty well executed, but a fake nonetheless."

The car enters the small hamlet of Barbizon. The ivy-covered stone houses embrace the narrow street. We arrive at Hôtellerie du Bas Brèau and manage to park, half up on the curb.

It is lunchtime, and after registering – Brit had made a reservation – we repair to the dining room, approached by a gravel walk through a garden, where a sumptuous *salade Niçoise* and a bottle of champagne prepares us for a sensuous nap in a luxurious room on the second floor of the charming inn.

In the late afternoon, we sit in the garden among the flowers of May. Brit has brought his sketchpad with him, and he proceeds to draw my face with a bit of black charcoal. "I don't know about this," I tease him.

"You don't even have to look at it. It's for me," he teases back.

"Of course I want to see it! To know how you see me."

"Well, maybe I'll let you take a quick look-see," and he hands over his sketchpad.

I am touched. His view of my face is drawn so tenderly that as I return it to him I lean across and kiss him on the lips.

We dine later, this time roast partridge. We have more champagne. We stroll down streets and explore the art galleries and shops that line those streets. We sleep again, entwined in our luxurious bed. We spend Saturday with more of the same, for me in a haze of sensuality. We decide to stay another night, finally returning to Paris on late Sunday afternoon.

To a noisy maelstrom of activity!

The car can hardly drive down the avenue to Hotel Marcel. The traffic is meshed together, tightly packed. Included are a number of stretch limousines, cable news trucks, a van of photographers, who jump to the pavement and walk forward to the hotel, The Majestic. I had forgotten that tonight, Sunday, May 24th, is the grand opening.

We decide to park on a side street two blocks over and walk. The pavement is crowded and finally, we reach the entrance of my small hotel. Jean-Luc is standing on the stoop, relaxed, curious, talking with Sasha, who has camera in hand.

"*Allo*, you two. Here to join the turmoil?"

"I guess we have no choice," Brit says, and we all laugh, as René Poignal emerges from inside Hotel Marcel.

"What's the joke?" the policeman asks, with a nod to me.

"It's just such a mess," I say. "Any news of Kurt?"

"Oh, yes," and as he says this a white stretch limousine arrives at the front of the equally white *façade* of the hotel next door.

"I'll fill you in tomorrow. There's much to tell." René whispers, distracted by the ongoing scene.

From the enormous automobile, an apparent sheik, Emir, Arab dignitary of some sort, emerges, in flowing robes and white head cover. Two bodyguards in dark suits, precede him. In the rear, following him, are three women in head-to-toe black burkas, totally covered except for docile brown eyes peering out from each hidden face. They too are accompanied by two bodyguards. The Emir – whosoever he may be - enters The Majestic with a royal stride.

Sasha, of course, is snapping pictures of this dramatic scene. "Wait 'til tomorrow – when all this hullabaloo is finished. I'll be able to get some beauts!"

"I understand the Emir has taken the whole top floor. The building is no taller than mine – six floors high – but there are four royal suites up there - that's what they call them – 'royal suites.'"

Jean-Luc lets out a scoffing laugh. "Royal, indeed."

"Are you worried about the competition?" René asks, his voice remarkably gentle.

"Not at all," says my hotelier. "*Au contraire*. I relish it. We have the same superior location. And mine has a certain small charm, while The Majestic is so elaborate it could be in any part of the world – Dubai, Hong Kong."

"Indeed there's no doubt that Hotel Marcel is in Paris!" Brit exclaims. And we all nod in agreement.

"Besides," Jean-Luc continues. "Let's not forget about the price! My fees are at least one-tenth the cost of any room over there...or even less. And if my clientele should want to live it up for a moment, they can always walk a few feet to an elegant bar – a chef inspired restaurant – then quietly return to a very inexpensive *lit et petit déjeuner chez moi* – to recover."

"The best of both worlds," Brit says. "You've got it made, Jean-Luc." He pauses. "I hate to leave all of you, but I must," and he takes my hand and pulls me into the lobby which is empty. Standing there together, he takes me in his arms and whispers, "The loveliest week-end of my life."

"Me too, darling," I whisper back. And with a quick "I'll call you," my Brit is gone this night.

# Chapter 32

❧

## A Day Full of Busy-ness

After breakfast, downstairs, on Monday morning, Jean-Luc tells me that René Poignal will be in the hotel around 11:00 o'clock. He is sure I will like to hear the latest information regarding Kurt and Jillian. Of course, I am most eager to know what is going on. It seems my nature demands answers.

In the meantime, I decide to stroll around the neighborhood to see the remnants of the grand opening last evening next door – if there are any. Are the reporters still on the street, and how about TV trucks?

No. It appears quite calm on the avenue, but it is still early. The day has only just begun. But I see Sasha across the street, munching on a bit of *baguette*. I pick my way through traffic and join him on the sidewalk opposite The Majestic. It is a little after 10:00.

We say our good mornings, and as we do, we see a white stretch limousine pull up to the entrance. Two bodyguards, interchangeable in looks, exit the grand hotel, and behind them the three burka-clad ladies emerge. Sasha snaps a picture. "Just in case," he says, as the women enter the vehicle, the two men jumping in as well. The huge car moves off into traffic.

"Some retailer is going to be mighty happy," Sasha remarks through munches.

"Now, don't be cynical," I say. "Those ladies deserve a day out in Paris, I'm sure. I wonder what they'll buy."

"Probably very expensive household items – you know – Limoges china, bed linens from Porthault, that kind of stuff."

"Oh look," I say, as another limousine arrives, this one black. Again, two men step out, obvious bodyguards, different from the ones accompanying the burka wives, but equally interchangeable.

Two stylish but underdressed young women then get out of the automobile, earrings dangling, faces lipsticked, bright blonde, bright redhead, stiletoes clicking. They giggle their way into the grand hotel. The bodyguards follow.

"Well what do you know!" Sasha says with a huge grin. "I got a really good couple of pix out of that little scene."

"The Emir is obviously a very busy fellow," I say, smiling too at this mini-drama taking place on this suddenly no longer quiet street.

I look across toward Hotel Marcel where I see Jean-Luc on the stoop. He has apparently also seen the two ladies–in–business as they entered The Majestic. When he sees me, he smiles and waves, as René Poignal rounds the corner.

"Gotta go, Sasha," I say. "Keep an eye out."

"You can bet on it. I ain't goin' anywhere," and he leans back against the corner of a building with an air of satisfaction, and calmly finishes the *baguette*.

Jean-Luc ushers René and myself into his office and shuts the door with a flourish.

Before I can sit down, René announces, "The brute is in custody."

"You're kidding!" I am astounded it all happened so quickly.

"Yes. The leash, which you pointed out, well, we found it

hanging near the door of the salon...can you imagine...so *flagrant*...
right out in the open. It was still damp...the leather...where he'd
tried to wash it...and the studs, there were traces of blood and even
*tissu humain*..."

"I guess he didn't clean it very well, eh?" remarks Jean-Luc.
"*Quelle bête!*"

"According to Sylvie...when you could get her to stop crying...
Kurt had let himself into the apartment that night...very late...
about 2:00AM, she thought... Emile woke up...and the two men
had a terrible fight in the middle of the master bedroom... Emile
accusing Kurt of ruining his chances with Isabella and how he'd
cost him money...and how he had never been anything but trouble.
Sylvie, who came in from the guest room, says she managed to get
Kurt to go with her down to the salon even though he was very
drunk..."

"I'm beginning to feel sorry for Sylvie," I say.

"Well don't," René continues. "Don't bother. Anyway, Kurt,
I gather, got more and more angry and grabbed the leash and ran
upstairs. She collapsed in the salon, but hearing a crash of glass,
she went upstairs and found her husband dead on the floor of the
bedroom, his neck a sea of blood surrounded by glass shards from
the long dressing mirror smashed to pieces. Kurt either threw him
into it or Emile fell."

"And Kurt?" I ask.

"He disappeared into the night. But once we got a hold of the
leash...not until the next day after he had washed it and walked the
dog – funny how habits never die – we had it tested and we went
to the apartment and took him in. Surprisingly, he was very quiet."

"Whew. What a saga," I say.

"He'll be going away for a very long time."

All three of us are silent in the little office.

"Oh, by the way," says René. "Your friend Jillian. I found out her maiden name was Helen Cadwell. She did marry a Spenser... she got pregnant, but before the girl baby was born, they were divorced. I guess she keeps the name Spenser because it sounds more elegant in England than being a... Cadwell."

"Poor little Amelia." I think of Duke. Maybe he can help his little friend although I have no idea how.

"Oh, apparently the father is a decent sort. He pays child support. It's not much apparently, but it shows responsibility. He doesn't see much of his daughter, particularly now that she's in France."

"I doubt the father even knows where she is," I say mournfully. "And the picture? The Corot?"

"I alerted Drouot. They are prepared for her. In fact, the painting should be over there to be appraised on Wednesday. She made an appointment. The auction's on Thursday at noon. I'll be there."

"Maybe I will too," I say.

"We'll see. Don't know that's such a good idea. We don't know what to expect of her."

Jean-Luc has been silent through the whole session with René Poignal. His head has been turning like he's at a tennis match. As we prepare to leave, he takes me to the door and says, "A lot to absorb, *non?*"

"*Mais oui*," I say with a sigh. René shakes my hand and says, "*Merci* for your help. And your information did help...oh yes, *vraiment.*"

I smile wanly, thinking of the lost, sad people whose machinations have brought so much mayhem and sorrow. Amelia. That poor little girl.

I step out of the hotel on the street, to get some fresh air and clear my spinning head. I see Sasha, still waiting at his post across the street. I decide to join him for a moment. He always amuses. I need cheering up.

He greets me happily. "I've been here two hours. It's getting boring, but I'd bet something juicy will come along."

"How do you know that," I say.

"Just say, instinct." And, in fact, at that moment, his two-hour wait is rewarded. We see the two young 'ladies-of-business', followed by the bodyguards, come out of The Majestic. They get into a waiting town car. The bodyguards stay on the pavement but see the women into the automobile, both girls looking completely satisfied, delighted with whatever recompense they have received.

Sasha is snapping away compulsively with his camera, when the white limo arrives and the three burka-clad ladies descend from the automobile. (Fortunately, the town car has left the premises.) They are animated, brown eyes no longer docile but excited as they leave the automobile. They laugh together. They carry large, expensive paper bags, on each of which is printed in grand cursive script in red ink, the name of the store. Victoria's Secret.

Who knew!

All of a sudden, the two bodyguards spot Sasha who has moved closer to capture the scene, flashbulbs blinking. They yell at him, rush toward him, but Sasha is young and agile and manages to weave his way across the street again through moving traffic, and disappear down a side street, precious camera with its load of goodies in his care.

Sasha has not been a photographer in war zones for nothing!

Victoria's Secret. Well, I'll be.

# Chapter 33

❦

## The End in Sight

Tuesday and Wednesday go by in a blur of activity; phone calls, lunches, dinners. I am painfully aware that my visit is coming to an end, with the airplane flight to New York City on the coming Sunday. So few days left. So many dramas to close. So little time to be with Brit.

On Tuesday I have arranged a final lunch with Sue, at, of course, *Caviar Kaspia*. Over superb poached eggs on croutons, topped with red salmon roe, I tell Sue of my concern for Amelia.

"Tomorrow Jillian is taking the Corot to be appraised at The Drouot Auction House."

"I know of it," Sue says. "Very prestigious."

"René Poignal, the detective – has alerted them that the painting may well be a forgery. On Thursday around noon, the Corot is due to be auctioned off – but the police will be there – if the picture's fake – to pick up Amelia's mother and take her into custody. Can you imagine the trauma for her daughter? That poor child!"

"That's truly awful," says Sue. "What will happen to the little girl? Where will she go?"

"God knows. She does have a father in England, and I suppose they will contact him. It's a strange story. Apparently, Jillian divorced Spenser when she was pregnant with Amelia – so the child hardly knows her father...never lived with him."

"It's strange," Sue says thoughtfully. "Somewhere it sounds familiar."

"What do you mean?"

"Well, who does it remind you of?"

"Who?"

"Think, Elizabeth. Think."

I pause over the delicious soft egg yolk with its bright, briny beads on top. I drop my fork. "Duke!"

"Yes, Duke. He lost his mother. She died. He never knew his father – and now he does – and you told me their reconciliation is moving along. He might be of some help to the girl. You said they like each other."

"Duke," I repeat. "He might be the only one who can help her...if she will let him in. It didn't occur to me...but it's worth a shot. I know he would like to...but it's up to her..."

"Better warn him soon. It looks like this will come down quickly."

"Oh, I will. You're brilliant, Sue. I'm sure Duke will want to help Amelia. He really is fond of her."

Back in my room at the hotel, after a teary good-bye to Sue, and an extra shot of vodka for us both, I lie on my bed for a little rest when the phone rings. It is a strange, French-tinged woman's voice, saying tentatively, "Elizabeth?"

"Yes," I reply.

"It is Elise Frontenac here."

I sit up abruptly. "Yes, Elise."

"I am calling... Pierre and I...we are having a small dinner party on Friday night and we wished you might join us. If possible."

"That sounds lovely. Why yes, I would be pleased to come to your *diner*. And thank you for asking me."

Elise clears her throat. "We are having the *diner*...to...introduce Pierre's son from America...well, to acknowledge..."

"I understand. I know Duke will be very happy that you honor him in this way," I say, trying to help the lady in her flustered state. "I would love to be part of it."

"Around 8:00?"

"Excellent. I'll be there, and thank you again."

She rings off.

As I pick up a *tranche* of *paté de campagne* at *Le Nôtre,* a green salad and a half-bottle of *Pinot Noir* for my supper, I wonder what remarkable dessert we will dine on Friday evening. I know Henriette is a cook, but she always seems to buy baked delicacies from this particular amazing store.

I also purchase four long gift boxes of macaroons (*macarons* in French) to bring home to New York City next Sunday for three particular friends.

The fourth one is for me.

Wednesday is a continued blur of activity involving preparations for my trip home...final plans with Brit. He and I are to dine tonight. We will be together all day on Saturday. And he wants to accompany me to the airport on Sunday morning. It will be so hard to leave him. I cringe at the thought.

# Chapter 34

## The Majestic

Around 6:00 in the early evening, I await Brit downstairs in the lobby, wearing my black dress (which he loves.) As he enters to collect me, Jean-Luc and Isabella appear from his office. As Brit and I turn to leave, Jean-Luc calls out, "*Eh bien*, you two. How about having a drink with us at the hotel next door?"

Brit and I exchange glances as if to say 'what hotel?' because even the idea of it is so new. Then we start to laugh and say in unison, "Great idea."

As we approach The Majestic, I look up at the balconies of the four royal suites on the sixth floor. Each one has a pot of red carnations, and strangely enough, a small palm tree. But, after all, Jean-Luc has told me that the conglomerate owning The Majestic is from Qatar, the richest per capita oil producing country in the world. Also the smallest. So, of course a palm tree is *de rigueur*.

My balcony may not have a palm tree, but it surely does have the same view at a pittance of the cost of a Majestic room. The Eiffel Tower.

The lobby of The Majestic is immense, with blindingly white walls, and black and white square tiles make up the slippery floor.

Onyx? Alabaster? It reminds me of the linoleum floor in a kitchen of my youth.

At the far end of the lobby is a black marble registry desk, flanked by two white columns to the ceiling. Behind it stands a tall, supercilious-looking gentleman in a dark uniform. We move towards him and realize he recognizes Jean-Luc, for he extends a hand and says, "Monsieur Marcel, I believe," in a strong British accent.

"Welcome to the Majestic," he continues as Jean-Luc shakes his hand. "I hope you will be bringing more guests as the months go by," nodding at Isabella, Brit, and myself. "We have an excellent Japanese chef in the *''Fusion'* dining room..."

Leaving this gentleman in mid-sentence, Brit leans to me and whispers, "He has some superiority complex," at which I nod. We make our way over to the bar on the left of the grand entrance doors. This room has a tent-like draped ceiling. There are a number of black tables with tiny lamps, red velvet banquettes, and round stools to pull up with red leather tops. A pretty oriental girl comes over and takes our order for a bottle of *Sauvignon Blanc*.

Our wine arrives.

"The whole place is ugly," Brit says looking around intently. "It's so dark. And not a painting or piece of art anywhere. It's unreal." He sips the wine, shaking his head in dismay. "Do you realize there is absolutely nothing of Paris here? Why, we could be anywhere in the world – even Qatar, for God's sake – and not know what country we are in!"

"Isn't it marvelous?" Jean-Luc bursts out. I can tell he is exuberant. "It's great for Hotel Marcel. Most people who come to Paris, want things French. That's why they're here. *Chez moi*, they can have that experience. You know my pictures in the lobby – the ones of the various stages of the building of the *Tour Eiffel* – and

the photos of Maurice Chevalier and Yves Montand in the salon."
Jean-Luc is beaming.

"True," I say. "And it's cold here, no warmth at all. I'm glad we
came. There is nothing of France or French in this 'grand hotel.'
Why, it's a hotel without a country."

"Well said, Elizabeth! There is nothing French *ici, pas chez* The
Majestic, évidemment …but just down the street…now there's a
small hotel…" and Jean- Luc is laughing. "Not here…but there.
There's Paris. Thank God."

# Chapter 35

## Final Brush Strokes

It happened. It really happened. I was not there, but on his return to Hotel Marcel, early this afternoon, René Poignal relates to Jean-Luc and me the scene that had taken place at the Drouot Auction House this Thursday noon.

Apparently, it was high drama.

When Corot's '*Nymphe en Rose*' appeared on an easel on the stage, with a starting price of 80,000 euros, the bidding started in earnest. Jillian was seated on the aisle in the third row from the rear of the auditorium, with Amelia at her side. Both were highly excited.

When the gavel finally came down, the buyer, a heavy woman from Brazil, stood to claim her prize, only to be approached by the auctioneer, prepared to apprise her of the truth.

At the same time, René and two policemen came to Jillian's side and quietly escorted her to the hallway next to the exit of the building, followed by a confused and upset little girl.

"I told Jillian Spenser I had to take her in, that the Corot was a proven forgery, that we had been in touch with Interpol," René began, in his account to Jean-Luc and myself. We are in Jean-Luc's office, as usual.

"You know, that woman is amazing. She didn't bat an eye. She kind of shrugged her shoulders, as if to say, 'at least I tried.' I had a policewoman take her over to the station for arraignment."

"And the little girl?" I ask anxiously. I had spoken to Duke earlier about Amelia's predicament. He is deeply concerned.

"Where is she? How is she?"

"Well, of course she's in a state. I brought her back to the apartment across the street with another policewoman – a young one and very *sympathique*. I'm headed over there now."

"Can I come?" I ask. Jean-Luc echoes my request.

"You both deserve to."

"And Duke? He should come too. He has befriended Amelia more than any of us…"

René looks quizzical. "I guess it's okay," and Jean-Luc calls upstairs and speaks to the young man in the room next to mine.

René, Jean-Luc and I cross to Jillian's duplex building. We arrive at the fourth floor.

Amelia is sitting on a chair in the corner, arms wrapped around her knees, disconsolate. Her face is pale, her eyes fearful, with dark shadows below the lower lids.

At Drouot, there had been much crying between mother and daughter as Jillian was led away by a policewoman. "Mommy, no," the child had wailed. "No, no, no," but to no avail. "My girl, the law is the law," René had expounded. "And your Papa is more than ready to take you in."

René goes to her now in this room and speaks softly to her, telling her that tomorrow she will be taken by a caretaker to the Chunnel train station, where she will board the train to London to be met there by her father who has been informed of the fate of his ex-wife and is prepared to embrace his young daughter.

I see that Duke has arrived. He has been watching this. He does not take his eyes off the little girl. As we leave to go to the fifth floor – a place about which I am immensely curious – I see Duke approach her, kneel down next to her chair and gently take her hand.

"It looks like a factory up here," René Poignal is saying as we enter the fifth floor of Jillian's duplex. Duke and Jean-Luc, with the young policewoman, stay below with Amelia.

"Jillian never let anyone up here," I remark. "A factory but pretty well organized. See, over here are the smaller old canvasses in a stack. The larger ones are on the other side of the room, over there."

Centered is an easel on which there is a partially finished Matisse '*Odalisque.*' It is eerie how truly similar Jillian's copy is to the original, almost an exact replica. "No wonder she got away with fraud for as long as she did," I say.

"And look," the detective says, pointing to a larger canvas on the floor, leaning against the wall, that is an obvious Chagall copycat, partially complete.

In the far corner of the big room, next to an extra-sized sink, there is a counter on which rest a number of cans of turpentine, two well-worn scrub brushes, a scraper tool with bits of paint stuck to the blade, and several discolored sponges.

"She strips them – the old canvasses – seasons them by drying..." René says, as if talking to himself. He opens the door to an inner room, which is equipped like a small library, with art books in disarray, a desk with a lap-top computer, printer, and fax machine. With all her air of innocence and artlessness, Jillian Spenser is highly sophisticated, at least in terms of her calling: forgery.

We descend to the fourth floor. René sends the policewoman upstairs to bag certain items the detective designated with small, numbered squares of paper. He then walks off with Jean-Luc to discuss the latest discoveries.

Duke is still kneeling next to Amelia. He calls her name. She does not speak.

"Amelia, it's going to be all right. Really. You'll see." Duke speaks gently.

"But I barely know my father," the girl suddenly bursts out. "I've only seen him a few times in my whole life...and when I was really young," and she starts to cry again.

Duke pulls some tissues from a box on the table that the policewoman had placed there for Amelia. He hands them to her, but first, takes one Kleenex to touch her cheek where drops had fallen. "I promise you, it will get better," he says. "I know what you're feeling. But you'll be surprised," and then, "I know I was."

"What do you mean you were surprised?" Amelia cries out angrily. "You never lost your mother and had to go to a man who happened to be your father who you never really knew. How could you know what I'm feeling?"

"Because it happened to me too...oh, not exactly...but mostly... the same thing...only my momma died and I never even knew who my father was...until now, I found him and ...well, it's all good..."Amelia is looking at him intently.

"Hey, I got something for you." And from his backpack, which is on the floor beside him, he pulls a small bag of macaroons. "Here, this should make you feel a little better." With that gesture, Amelia throws her arms about his neck. "Oh Duke, will you come with me to the train station tomorrow? You know, I'm scared."

"Don't be frightened, little girl. I'll come with you to the station and give you a happy farewell. Now eat up before these things melt."

"They don't melt, silly," And for the first time, Amelia smiles.

# Chapter 36

❧

## Diner Chez Frontenac

The sultry sound of Billie Holiday wafts through the dining room, subtly reminding Duke of his mother's voice. Friday night. We are six at table; Jean-Luc and Isabella, our hosts, Pierre and Elise Frontenac, Duke Pierre Davis and me.

Fat white asparagus from Belgium, with *sauce hollandaise*, is our first course, followed by salmon filets with a pale mustard glaze and small boiled potatoes in brown butter.

The wine is a spectacular *Pouilly Fuissé* which loosens tongues, lifts spirits, and makes for a mellow mood.

I am overwhelmed by the copacetic atmosphere that prevails at Elise's restored antique dining table. Tonight, our hostess is softer than I have ever seen her. She is deferential to Duke, even boasting of his talent. "Duke's treatment of the violin…his amazing use of his bow…it is a delight to hear," she says, beaming at the young man sitting at her right.

I have forgotten how much music means in the Frontenac world. If Duke had happened to be a scholar or a lawyer or a plumber, his reception by the pair might have been very different.

But his musicianship and love of music has given the three of them something in common, deep to share, and constant to love.

Henriette reappears with salad of delicate greens dressed in lemon.

She also places an elaborate cheese board –*Brie, Roquefort, Stilton*– with a variety of breads – on the table, plus another chilled bottle of the elegant wine.

Pierre rises to his feet at the end of the table. He lifts his glass. "I want to make a toast to the good friends here tonight, and especially to the young man I never knew as my son until now."

"Here, here," I say. And we all sip the golden liquor.

"I want him – and all of you – to know what Duke brings to our life. I admire his determination to find his father – in fact, I bless it – his need to know who <u>he</u> is – by knowing me." Pierre chokes a little. "Most important, he gives us – Elise and me – a family we never had. We didn't realize what that means until he came to us. Welcome, my son," and he raises his glass in Duke's direction before he sits down.

Elise is dabbing her eyes with her napkin, as Henriette appears to clear the table. We sit in silence, all of us quite overcome by the emotion of the moment. She reappears with a beautiful *gâteau au citron*, (from *Le Nôtre*) decorated with white flowers made of sugar.

I find it hard to believe that Pierre and Elise Frontenac, whom I had assumed to be as stuffy and rigid, as uncompromising as it is possible to be, have the heart and generosity to accept Duke as their own.

But they do. They have. They humble me. I have learned a major lesson about being so judgmental.

As the evening draws to a close and we collect our belongings to go across the street to Hotel Marcel, Duke catches me as I enter the corridor to the elevator. "Thank you, Elizabeth."

"Oh, Duke, you don't have to thank me. They are coming to love you. It's obvious your father needs you, in fact."

"You made it possible."

"No, no, Duke. You did – because you're the way you are," and I lean over and kiss him on the cheek. "Goodbye for now. I'm off Sunday – back to New York, but I'll be in Paris for Christmas. Until then."

Jean-Luc, Isabella and I find our way home to my small hotel. We are quiet. Jean-Luc then tells me that he had brought Amelia to stay overnight in a room at Hotel Marcel. "Poor little one had no place to go. Then today the policewoman came and she took her to the train station."

"Didn't Duke go with them?" I ask anxiously.

"*Oui*, he did. He took her by the hand and even paid for a taxi to take them there."

"I knew he would. He really identifies with that little girl. Two of a kind."

I go upstairs, and before I go to bed, I step out on my balcony and look up at the Eiffel Tower. It stands tall and proud as always. Seeing it I feel only contentment in my heart, and alive with the awareness of how truly good some people can be.

# Chapter 37

$\backsim \text{\textcircled{·}} \backsim$

## A Paris Saturday


And one to remember. Brit and I spend it in the Marais district, in the Place des Vosges, and in the narrow bed of his studio. It goes by so fast, this day of sensuality –promises promised – wine to be drunk – music to be heard – and love to be loved.

He is going to London in a few days. There is to be a show of his work at a gallery near Hampshire Gate, a rather posh part of that great city. He will be there for at least a week. "Come with me," he begs, but I must go home. It has been a month that I have been away, already more time than expected by me and those in New York City who depend on me.

Brit expects to come to my hometown in October, yet another exhibit, sponsored by American Vogue. Ray Guild is again behind this.

"Just remember that I will be working full out in the next weeks and months. I have to supply more product for not one, but two shows!" Brit is invigorated by the thought of the events themselves, the work in progress, the exciting venues to travel, and then, there is me. He makes that very clear. "You, Elizabeth. You are the jewel at the end of the road."

His words send me into orbit.

Saturday, late, he takes me back to the Hotel Marcel. On the stoop of Hotel Marcel, I turn to him. "Don't come tomorrow morning."

Brit recoils, steps back. "Why not? I want to take you…" but I interrupt and say, "Leave me tonight." I <u>have</u> to say what I'm saying. "I am so full of you…I want to leave Paris with the warmth and the beauty of this day and night. In the cold of tomorrow morning…? No, no! Remember darling. The shortest farewells are the best." And with a long kiss, I leave him there on the stoop, looking quite bereft.

Upstairs, I tenderly place my precious *'Diamants,'* carefully wrapped in tissue paper, in the center of my suitcase between sweaters. I then finish packing the rest. I sleep a bit, and early Sunday morning, organize my shoulder bag for the flight home; passport, ticket, small pill case, a paperback to read, some mints, a bunch of tissues. Mounir, the driver is to pick me up here at the hotel around 10. My flight is at 1:00.

I go out on the balcony to greet a sunny sky and glance across at the LaGrange apartment to see an unexpected sight. Sylvie Vronsky LaGrange. The shades on the salon windows are up, and Sylvie is there with a large coffee cup in hand. She wears a resplendent red satin robe.

Most astonishing is her red hair. It is cut in a chic bob that seems to lengthen her neck and make her cheeks look less plump. I run in and grab the binoculars which I have yet to pack, and fix my gaze on Sylvie.

She looks positively radiant. There is nary a tear stain on her face, and I notice on the back wall there is a brand new leash for Schnitzel. It too is bright red.

Looks to me like a new merry widow has just arrived in town!

# *Epilogue*

❦

## The shortest farewells are the best

Ludwig Turner, artist and lover, my Brit
Jean-Luc Marcel and Isabella
Duke Pierre Davis
Pierre and Elise Frontenac
Sasha Goodman
Ray Guild
Sue de Chevigny
Sylvie Vronsky LaGrange – merry widow
Little English girl – Amelia Spenser
René Poignal, intrepid sleuth

In Jail: Kurt Vronsky
Jillian Spenser
Dead: Emile LaGrange

Quite a roster to come back to. Quite a history to continue. What fresh drama will occur? And what new characters to bear witness?

As long as Brit is still in the Marais,
As long as The Majestic caters to Emirs,
As long as Sasha takes photos that matter,
As long as *Caviar Kaspia* stays in business,
As long as Isabella loves Jean-Luc,
As long as Sue's château still crumbles,
As long as the Eiffel Tower still reigns,

I will be back.

*Bien sûr*!